THE HENTY

THE HENTY

by

F. M. GRAVATT

VICTORY PRESS

LONDON and EASTBOURNE

Printed in Great Britain for
VICTORY PRESS (Evangelical Publishers Ltd.),
Lottbridge Drove, Eastbourne, Sussex,
by Richard Clay (The Chaucer Press), Ltd.,
Bungay, Suffolk.

CONTENTS

CHAPTER ONE

JAY, VINCE, AND THE HENTY

Jay Lewis gripped the sash window, waiting in case its squeaky movement had revealed the fact that he was not in bed. From downstairs he could hear the hum of his grandmother's sewing-machine, and, though his father had long since left for the night shift at Ellis's motor works, yet caution was a necessary part of any plan to outwit one's elders.

Outside the air was cool to his face and arms as he emerged from the box-like bedroom of seven Fortune Row. It was not yet dark; the trees that bordered the river beyond the gardens loomed shadowy against the evening sky. The silent presence of the river drew him. There, he and Vincent Collins had spent the long summer holidays, idling away the morning hours, doing nothing in particular, safe from any adult questions or criticism. Now the holidays were over, the holidays in which each of them had reached his twelfth birthday. The autumn term had begun.

Ducking his head under the half open window, Jay lifted one leg onto the sill. Then, with a last look into the room, to the clothes heaped to resemble his own sleeping form, he withdrew the other leg, and sat for a moment on the stone sill. He rested his plimsolled feet on the grey slates that formed the kitchen roof which jutted out beyond the rest of the small house, and surveyed the gardens. They were empty of workers, the fading light having driven them indoors. The gardens now held no danger; that could only come from within the ten houses that comprised Fortune Row.

Carefully closing the window, he began the descent, bending low lest he should be detected. Having gained the edge of the roof he stepped gingerly onto the narrow wooden beam that formed the lintel of the garden gate, straightening up in order to retain his balance on this narrow bridge which linked the roofs. Before he reached number ten he saw Vince's leg astride the window-sill. The Collins family lived in the last house in the row. Against its kitchen was erected a long, narrow shed whose roof continued the slope of the kitchen roof, making it a simple matter for the two to descend to the garden. Once in the garden Jay and Vince kept in the shelter of the fence till they reached the back gate that led to the path by the river. Vince had made sure that it was left unbolted, so that their exit was soundless. The gate from the Lewises' garden had been nailed up; for Jay's grandmother argued that, though it let you out, it might also let others in, and you never knew nowadays who was around.

Once by the river, there was no longer the same need to watch. No-one ever came along the path at night; no-one, of course, except themselves.

Jay laughed. "We did it. Told you." He sprang up and lunged at an overhanging tree.

Neither was tall for his twelve years. Jay was fair and well-built, while Vince, thin and wiry, had dark hair and almost black eyes. They trod cautiously, the sound of their feet hardly breaking the quiet. Henty's

Farm bordered the other side of the river, and at one time there were occasional anglers perched at intervals along the bank. Now the farm was sold and closed, and the new road was to cut across the south fields. Yet it was the sale of the farm that had given Jay and Vince the boat that had supplied most of their pleasure during the holiday. Wherever he had gone, Mr Henty had obviously no need of the small rowing-boat, or he would have taken it with him. Nor, they reasoned, had he sold it, or the buyer would have come for his purchase. So they had taken the boat and called her *The Henty*.

Jay halted by the trunk of a chestnut tree from where he could see the humped bridge with its three arches, under which they hid *The Henty*. Obscured by the profuse willow-herb that flourished on the bank, no ordinary passer-by would have suspected the presence of a boat. Nevertheless they were always anxious until they set eyes on her. Inside was their amateur fishing tackle, two supple bamboo rods from whose ends dangled lengths of twine.

"You seen the rod in Bakers?" asked Vincent.

"Yeh."

"Guess it ain't worth that." To both, the sum asked was exorbitant, for they knew, in different ways, the impossibility of ever acquiring something so expensive.

"It's better 'n Stan's," added Vince. Seventeen-year-old Stanley Richards lived at the other end of Fortune Row, and, though he declined to take any notice of them, they observed most of his doings.

"She's there O.K.," whispered Jay.

They knelt by the bridge, while Vince pulled at the rope that secured *The Henty*. The sound of its movement in the water excited Jay. "We ought to catch something tonight," he said.

Inexpert at fishing, together they could throw their lines on to the waiting stream as though they had the most expensive gear and the talent to use it. In each other's company, here, by the deserted reaches of the Ander, they could practise with complete freedom, till one day they would emerge practised and efficient, and be at ease in front of others.

"Wish I'd got one of them lines like Stan's." Vince aped the action, sensing the pull of the imaginary line, hearing the sound of the reel.

Jay laughed. Vince was a comic when he took off other people; his face was as mobile and quick as a clown's. He scrambled into the boat, while Vince held it to the shore. Now, for a brief spell, there was the river with its darkening water, the all-absorbing occupation of fishing, and then they must face the return journey, and the consequences if they were caught. For Jay it would mean the tiresome job of explaining and enduring his father's regret that he couldn't give his son the exciting holidays other boys had. For Vince it would be meeting his parents' sharp anger at his daring to go off.

And tomorrow they would meet as though they had never moved in the shadows of the overhanging trees, never rowed *The Henty* when they should have been indoors asleep.

CHAPTER TWO

THE MORNING AFTER

At the sound of his name, Jay flung off the clothes and sprang from bed.

"Coming," he sang out, then pulled back the curtains and took one look at the garden and the trees beyond. The excitement and mystery of the previous night had vanished; things were ordinary once more. Until their next nocturnal outing, he would not dream of making his exit by way of the window. It was marvellous to think that no-one had any idea what he and Vince had been doing. This morning he had been too sound asleep to hear his father come in from Ellis's, and now it was breakfast time. After dressing hastily Jay raced down to the kitchen.

"Hallo, Dad."

"Hallo, Jay."

As he sat down to breakfast he glanced at his grandmother, hoping she wouldn't comment on his lateness. Fortunately she was busy with preparing porridge, bacon and egg, crisp fried bread, her recipe for a vigorous day. The memory of last night's outing came back to him, with Vince in *The Henty*; and what he and Vince did was secret. Then he was conscious of his grandmother's eyes on him, as she moved empty plates, re-filled cups.

"I've put your sandwiches on your satchel," she

said. Since going to the secondary school in Lisham, and having to stay for school dinner, she had supplied him with a similar packet each morning, not trusting anyone else to provide him with enough to eat.

"Thanks, Gran." He said nothing about sharing the contents with Vince, lifting the corner of each sandwich to discover if it was to their liking.

Jay wiped the back of his hand across his mouth.

Always swift to get one task over and begin on the next, she was never in a hurry to release Jay. She sensed his air of excitement, his hastily combed hair, his eagerness to be off. Not wanting him to miss his mother, she tried to order his life, fill every moment of his time. But it was so long ago his mother had died, Jay had no memory of the old life, so how could he know what it was he had lost? Hovant with its deserted railway station, its river, its sleepy jumble of cottages and large houses was what he knew and depended on.

"It's Vince you're in such a hurry to meet," Gran remarked.

Jay was offended. It was the sort of remark which left him dumb, just waiting for enough time to pass for her to know he did not intend answering.

Mr Lewis folded the white table-napkin and inserted it into the silver ring engraved with the initials A.G.S.

"'Bye, Dad. 'Bye, Gran." He picked up his things in the hall and then made his way out into the front garden, brushing against the chrysanthemums that his grandmother was hoping to exhibit later in the year.

"Hey, Vince," he exclaimed.

Together they watched Stan Richards come from

the first house in the row and rev up the motor-bike which was now his transport to school. They knew he was out to impress them, but they accepted this as part of him. Sometimes they would catch sight of him at school with half a dozen others, arguing, or ambling along the corridor with his bulky brief-case tucked under one arm. Now he was off, bumping over the uneven road, the sound of his motor-cycle still with them, as Jay and Vince went on past Hovant Station, once a scene of bustle early in the morning.

"It's coming," yelled Vince, and they ran furiously towards the bus stop.

They had no qualms about pushing their way onto the bus in order to gain their favourite place on the top deck. From here Jay could glance back at the railway station, the useless station which still had an air of solidarity about its saffron-coloured brick and dirty windows. He settled into the corner seat, leaving Vince to take the outside.

Vince nudged Jay. "You make it O.K. last night?"

" 'Course," assured Jay confidently.

"Me too."

"My gran had to wake me this morning."

"Did she say anything?"

"Not much." It was one of those mornings when Jay was out to impress Vince. "My dad's going to write a book. About railways, about the stations that have been closed like ours."

"S'pose he was famous," suggested Vince.

The bus jerked to a start and soon Hovant Station was lost to view.

"There's a friend of his coming to take photographs." Jay was thinking of his father, vaguely hoping that some day all the fantastic information his father possessed might bring some reward.

"You didn't tell your dad about us going there."

"I'm not daft," replied Jay. Although Jay took little interest in his father's collection of railway tickets, he had a liking for the deserted station; he even liked the stale, musty smell that hung around the booking office.

"Bet we could tell him things." Vince held up his pass for the conductor to inspect.

"Yeh," laughed Jay.

"Will your dad get a lot of money for it?" Vince counted bank notes into his palm.

Jay frowned. "Dunno." Not in his memory had any of his father's ventures produced much financial reward; so he was irritated by Vince mentioning the matter. Only the hours at Ellis's brought in the crisp notes that his grandmother would accept with her curt, "Put them on the dresser."

Meanwhile there was the river, *The Henty*, the sandwiches in his satchel from which he could catch the smell of new bread.

CHAPTER THREE

THE STORM

Vince pressed his face against the window, watching the rain course down the grey slates, knowing that, now, Jay too would have abandoned all hope of going to *The Henty*. So there was nothing left but to go to bed, which, after the thought of guiding their boat through the dark waters of the Ander, was a very tame finish to the day. He unlatched the window, and let the rain drive into his bedroom. From downstairs came the sound of the television, while up here there was also the sound of the rain hitting the slates, and sending up sprays of water at its impact.

Thrusting his head out into the rain, and willing Jay to do likewise, he heard the distant thunder. When he saw Jay's fair head emerge from seven Fortune Row, he waved frantically as lightning illumined the sky. Vince spread his hands to the rain, then, as a louder clap of thunder came, held his hands over his ears and grimaced at Jay, who gesticulated in response, not daring to call lest his grandmother should overhear. The storm roused in him a feeling of anticipation, wanting the elements to do something spectacular, even something calamitous. Another clap, nearer, and the rain, as though in competition, increased.

Jay gazed out to the trees. The river which had

been low all the long, dry summer, would rise, and how would *The Henty* fare? Would she be safe beneath the bridge, or would the swollen Ander draw her out into the open stream where the rain would fill her? With the rest of Fortune Row indoors, he signalled his fears to Vince; all that concerned them was that *The Henty* should be safe.

Then Jay saw the white streak in the sky; not a straight affair like the railway lines, but like the lines on maps that marked out the river, twisting, branching, which reminded him that the map today had been good. Another crash of thunder and he failed to hear his grandmother open the door.

"Jay!" She was beside him, observing the excitement in his eyes, eyes lit that very moment by another fork of lightning.

"Hey, that was a good one." He knew she didn't care for thunder-storms, which gave him an advantage. She was about to reprove him; his hair was wet, and where he was leaning on the sill his pyjama sleeves were damp.

"Wish I was out in it," he bragged.

"I suppose Vince is at it as well." She knew there were a great many things you could dare together; things which, alone, you would never consider.

Jay leant out further in time to see Vince withdraw. Without warning, the storm leapt nearer, a magnificent display of white lightning followed by a deafening crash. Jay kept still, and the next moment another fork of lightning lit the sky above the trees. It was not the ensuing thunder that startled him—for that he was prepared—but the prolonged rending sound that followed in its wake.

"Please, God, let *The Henty* be safe," he prayed.

His grandmother could not conceal her dislike of the storm. Something happened to her when thunder was around; her normal commonsense was shaken by its unknown power. The lightning showed up the lines on her face. But it was the previous flash that Jay would never forget; the effect as it struck was sharp in his memory.

"That'll be one of the trees," he heard his grandmother say. "I'll make a cup of something."

It pulled him from the spectacle of the storm. "Yeh, lets. Wish Vince could have one." He leant out to see if Vince had re-appeared, expecting his grandmother to say, "That's all you think about", but she made no comment, and he, anxious to say something in Vince's favour, remarked, "He's fantastic at maths."

It roused her. "He beats you?"

" 'Course he does."

"Mm."

"I did a jolly good map today; got an A."

"Mm, your father was like that. I've still got his books. Never throw away a good piece of work. Now come on downstairs. The damp's not good for anyone. I could do with a cup of tea. Shut that window now."

Wanting to stay there and see the storm out, he was torn between that and a cup of cocoa and possibly a slice of buttered toast. But he followed her downstairs, keeping to the river of worn grey carpet that ran between the dark brown banks of polished wood either side, so that his bare feet did not feel the chilly impact of the floor. Here on the stairs the storm assumed a different character; here, enclosed and safe, you could be neither threatened nor excited by it. He followed his grandmother into the kitchen.

She rubbed her thin hands. "The summer's done," she declared, and he did not argue that it was only the beginning of September.

"We'll need a bit of warmth in the evenings." She continued to caress the backs of her hands, trying to bring some heat into them. Then Jay watched her setting out the china, filling the kettle. His father had slim, white hands with bluish veins that showed up like swollen streams and tributaries flowing from his wrist to his fingers. He began to think of his father's collection.

"Gran," he said at last, taking the cup of hot cocoa, "is it very valuable?"

"He doesn't appreciate how valuable," she said.

Queer how she read his thoughts; annoying, unless of course the storm had turned her mind to the safety of the precious items.

She sat down at the table. "He should get it insured."

"Why?" Jay was waiting for the toast. The enticing smell was already pervading the kitchen.

"Something you should do with valuable things. No good moaning afterwards. Always remember that."

"Oh." He spread his hands round the freshly made cup of cocoa, but it was too hot to keep them there.

"Then if anything happens, you have the money." Now she was spreading the butter with quick, short movements.

"What sort of things would happen?" Jay took the plate and considered the hot toast. It had been worth leaving the window after all.

"Theft, fire. And you could lose them yourself. Silly things happen."

"S'pose so."

"Now if that Victorian collection your grandfather started . . . if anything happened to that——"

"Dad would get the money. How much?" Jay bit into the warm, buttery surface.

"Whatever he'd insured for. You'll not understand that."

"I will," he retaliated. "And if something happened now, he wouldn't get a bean." But he couldn't visualise a fire in Fortune Row, or a burglar, or his father losing them. They were safe in the neat, partitioned trays, those hundreds of tickets that fascinated his father.

"Don't you worry, I've got them insured."

He looked up at her, admiring her action, yet a little doubtful whether she was right, for it seemed disloyal to do something his father had omitted to do. People often remarked she didn't look like a grandmother, with her close-cropped black hair, untinged by grey, clear blue eyes and quick speech.

"Now be getting back to bed," she ordered at last; "the worst of the storm's over."

Jay ran his finger over the melted butter on the plate. "O.K., but it was a rattling good storm."

Back in his own room he peered out into the garden. The rain was gentle now, the storm spent, and no lightning lit the sky, but somewhere beyond the fences of Fortune Row there would be a tree seared by a white flash and levelled by the power of the storm. Tomorrow he must find it; tomorrow he and Vince must make sure *The Henty* was safe.

CHAPTER FOUR

HIDDEN MESSAGES

Jay dressed quickly, alive with the prospect of searching out the stricken tree. To wait till after school was out of the question; by then others would have discovered it, and to be first mattered; it made all the difference. The vision of that blinding flash that caught the tree, the sound of the rending crash that told its doom came back to him. He had to go and find out. The thing was, should he wait for Vince? Would there be enough time if he waited for Vince? They had an understanding that neither of them called for the other; they merely arrived outside their houses in Fortune Row, waited a bit if they happened to be early or sauntered ahead to the bus stop.

Jay wanted to communicate the urgency of the matter to Vince, and yet somewhere in the corner of his mind he wanted to go on his own. Though it conflicted with his ardent loyalty to Vince, he decided to make it alone, to get away early, and, by way of the grassy strip that separated Stan Richards' house from the two shops further on, to reach the river.

Downstairs he waited by the table while his grandmother filled the teapot.

"Bit of a storm last night." Mr Lewis picked up the newspaper. "Some flooding at Anderbury when I came through."

"Not surprising." Jay's grandmother brought the teapot across to the table. "They're always promising something will be done, but that's as far as they get."

"It was terrific last night, Dad."

"I shouldn't wonder there's a tree down." Mrs Lewis inclined her head in the direction of the river.

"We heard it," continued Jay. Through the window that looked on to the garden he could see the rambler rose, its tiny leaves heavy with rain, and just below on the draining board was his packet of sandwiches, wrapped first in greaseproof paper and then in a plastic bag. So he wouldn't have to hang around waiting for them. Not that he ever did have to wait. They ate their meal in silence, Mr Lewis glancing from time to time at the paper.

Jay went up to the draining board and took the packet of sandwiches, then grinning boldly at his grandmother he went out into the hall. His satchel was hanging there all ready, but how to escape without some explanation, some argument? The kitchen door was wide open and he was in full view of his grandmother.

Two letters came through the letter-box with a loud snap, one a largish postal package, the other an airmail. Grabbing them from the doormat he returned to the kitchen, squinting at the writing on the airmail.

"It's for Gran."

She took it from him, turned it over and back again, then went across to the drawer for a slim knife to slit the edges neatly. Jay handed the other package to his father, went into the hall and out of view of his grandmother and drew the door shut behind him.

Seizing his cap, and slinging his satchel over his shoulder, he made for the front door.

" 'Bye," he shouted, slamming the door behind him.

He made his way to the end of Fortune Row. Here the grass was heavy with rain, so that before he reached the path by the river his shoes were sodden. A mist hung about the water, film-like, giving a feeling of unreality and solitude. He looked to the left, along the back fences of Fortune Row. No disaster had struck there; he knew whatever had happened was further afield to the right. As he set out in that direction his feet slithered in the mud that only hours ago was a hard, sun-baked path.

There was no need to travel far, for just before the humped bridge that spanned the river between Henty's Farm and the village of Hovant he saw the object of his search. It was the old hollow oak, its massive trunk split by the fall, one blackened, shrivelled branch showing where the lightning had felled the giant which blocked his path and his view of *The Henty*. Now that he knew which tree had been struck, he must find out if the boat was safe. He clambered onto the shattered tree which had fallen away from the river's edge, and stood astride the trunk between the branching roots laden with earth and the bigger branches with their foliage. If it had been one of the trees behind Fortune Row it would have smashed right through the fences. He considered the length of it, reckoning how near their house it might have come. Even in the patchy mist which hung around everything, he saw something orange lying in the cloven trunk just above the roots.

He looked right and left, *The Henty* forgotten, then stooped down to investigate.

Envelopes! Telegrams! Five, seven—— How did they get there? It was some dark mystery that last night's storm had uncovered, and he had discovered it. There was no time to look at them now; the thing was what to do. He had got here first, so he argued he had a right to them. Not a soul knew he was here.

Taking the sandwiches from his satchel, he removed them from the plastic bag, then carefully lifting each orange envelope, he placed them in the transparent cover. They smelt musty and woody, and he was afraid to handle them too much lest they tear. Who knew what he would reveal? *Jay Lewis finds long-lost messages, Jay*—— But now he must get to school. Retracing his steps by the side of the river, he then raced through to Fortune Row. There was no sign of Vince, so he ran on past Hovant Station.

Vince turned and saw him. "Where you bin?" he called, not angry, but curious.

Breathless, Jay looked up and down the road. Sure that no-one was within earshot, he leant across to Vince. "I found something." He patted his satchel.

Vince knew all the signs, the excitement, the air of secrecy. Jay was on to something, or else he had an idea, and that meant something for them to plan and to do. All of him responded to the thought of one of Jay's schemes. Tomorrow was Saturday; that meant freedom, time to spend on their own affairs, time for *The Henty*.

"What you found?" he asked, rubbing his nose.

Jay raced ahead, then stopped suddenly. "Tell

you what. You come to my place tonight." He
frowned. There was always the problem of being on
their own, of being a hundred per cent certain no-
one would interrupt them.

"O.K.," assented Vince.

"I'll ask my gran. You come to tea," decided Jay.
The hollow oak's down. I've just seen it."

"Bet that's smashed it a bit."

"Yeh, it's bust all right." He put his hand protec-
tively over the satchel. "Tell you tonight."

"We missed the first bus, I reckon," said Vince,
but neither of them was much concerned.

CHAPTER FIVE

SECRETS REVEALED

Once in the kitchen Jay's boldness began to desert him. You didn't tell Gran someone was coming to tea; you asked her. On the other hand there was a sure way of making her say yes, without actually asking her.

"Gran."

"Mm," she was busy ironing.

"Me and Vince've got something we want to do tonight."

"Oh."

"Where's Dad?"

"In the shed fixing the broken chair."

Jay thrust his hands in his pockets. "Vince is outside; we were deciding whether to go to his place."

Her eyes flashed. "You were deciding. You were not. Nothing of the sort. You asked Vince in to tea."

He pretended to be examining the sink.

"Go and tell the boy. Don't leave him standing outside."

It hadn't worked quite as he thought. "We want to go up to my room afterwards," he said sullenly.

"Goodness knows how you got your shoes in that state."

Jay surveyed his muddy shoes. Perhaps the truth was best. "I went down by the river to see which tree it was."

"Mm. Off with you and bring Vincent in."

"It was the hollow oak."

"So Mr Stanton told me when I went to get the bread. Should have been down a long time ago. Would you like sausages for tea?"

"Please." He was lighthearted. "I'll get Vincy."

They tore upstairs to Jay's room, impatient to open the long-hidden telegrams, for Jay had not been able to keep his secret through the day.

Jay's bed with its vivid orange cover was against the wall to the left of the door. The window opposite, through which he had escaped more than once to join Vince, also had bright orange curtains. Beneath the window Mr Lewis had fixed a collapsible work surface, which Jay now propped up with the wooden stays. A small cupboard and chest of drawers almost filled the remaining space. Jay spread a newspaper on the work surface, for he remembered the telegrams were soiled and damp, and he had no intention of leaving any marks which could give rise to questions. Vince drew up one of the chairs.

"See." Jay pointed out of the window. "It was just over there. Tell you what. We'll go and have a look in the morning."

"Sure." Vince was itching to get hold of the telegrams. "We got to do this first."

Jay placed the plastic bag on the table.

"S'pose someone comes up." Vince glanced at the door. Jay held on to the bag. His father always said goodbye before leaving for Ellis's, but there was a long time to go before then. And they had made it quite clear at teatime that they expected to be left on their own. "S'O.K.," he re-assured Vince; "we got plenty of time." He extracted the first envelope. "We got to do them carefully," he warned, seeing that Vince was in a hurry.

"Wonder who shoved them in that tree," queried Vince. "Anyone could've reached that hole easy."

"Bet you couldn't 've," laughed Jay.

"Would. I'd have got on your back, see."

Jay took out another of the envelopes and together they stared at the two addresses, one in Anderbury, the other in Lisham, both just names to them. If any thought of handing over the telegrams entered their minds neither mentioned the matter.

"We'll copy them," decided Jay, going across to a miniature set of drawers that stood on top of the cupboard. Once it had housed part of his father's ticket collection, and its intriguing compartments, and above all the fact that it had lock and key made it important to him. He extracted a biro and some writing paper and came back to Vince who could hardly keep his fingers from ripping open the telegrams.

Jay lifted the flap of the first envelope, the dampness making it comparatively easy, and began by reading the date.

"That's ages ago," Vince's voice rose in surprise.

"Ssh, they'll hear you," warned Jay.

Vince pretended to be communicating in deaf and dumb language; then, unable to keep silent, he asked, "What's it say?"

"Arriving 6.20 Euston. Two hours to spare. Meet me by the clock. David."

"S'pose he never went," surmised Vince.

" 'Course he never went." Jay was still looking at

the telegram. "He never got the message, so how would he know where to go."

"Might've been she," laughed Vince.

"Oh," said Jay. Altogether it was a depressing message, conjuring up David, David waiting and waiting for someone who failed to turn up.

"Where's it from?" Vince looked over Jay's shoulder. "Edinburgh," he read.

Jay put down the telegraph form. It felt limp and damp. "You write them out, and I'll put them back in the envelopes, afterwards." He unfolded the second telegram and read out, "Cancel all arrangements. Going in hospital. Letter to follow. Jackson." At least there would have been the letter in this case.

While Vince prepared to copy out the messages, Jay took out two more envelopes. A sudden rush o fear choked him, his fingers trembled. This was something he couldn't let Vince see; it was nothing to do with Vince. There it was: *Lewis, 7 Fortune Row, Hovant*. He let the envelope drop back into the plastic bag and selected another, hiding his confusion. Then he went across to the bed and with his back to Vince emptied the envelopes onto the orange cover. There it was again: *Lewis, Fortune Row*. He picked it up and deposited it safely in one of the small drawers and brought the remaining envelopes back to Vince.

"I've got an idea. Brains." Vince rolled his eyes. "What say you and me deliver them. Read them first, of course."

"Yeh, we will," agreed Jay; "they ought to have been delivered." The telegram addressed to his father—that ought to have arrived. Anger at the culprit made it easy for him to push aside the thought that what they were doing was not right.

"No-one must see us," Vince continued, while Jay's mind was still occupied with one particular telegram. "Bet there'll be a row."

"We'll fix it so no-one knows." Jay sat down beside Vince. He wanted there to be a row, he wanted someone to be punished. "We've got to keep them somewhere safe till we've got time to deliver them." Again he was aware that he should call a halt, but it was getting exciting, and the whole thing gave him a sense of power. "I'll put them in the drawer; I can lock it. No-one looks in there. It's mine."

"Hey, look at this one. It's for Mr Barnard." Vince was holding up one of the envelopes. They looked at each other, sizing up how the other felt about prying into the secrets of someone they knew, each unwilling to put the telegram aside. Mr Barnard ran the club for boys on Thursday evenings which Jay and Vince attended when they were in the mood. Jay prised open the envelope.

"We would do this one straight after church on Sunday, before Barney gets home," suggested Vince with glee. "That'll shake him."

Jay grinned, unfolding the paper. It was an errand after his own heart, getting people guessing, and all the time knowing the answer. They read the message that a year previous should have reached Mr Barnard.

Vince had gone. The telegrams, their messages copied in Jay's notebook, were now safely locked in the small drawer, and Jay was alone. Elated by his find earlier in the day, a little cocky that he and Vince possessed the means to startle people, he was uneasy that one of the telegrams was for his father.

What news, what calamity was concealed beneath the musty envelope? He sat on the edge of the bed, debating what to do about it. To hand it to his father did not fit in with the plans he and Vince had made; moreover it would mean divulging his find and surrendering the envelopes to the police or the post office. To give up the fun of secretly delivering the long-hidden messages, of getting everyone guessing, was more than he was prepared to do. It wouldn't be fair, he argued. And yet when he had said good-night to his father, half of him had wanted to share the secret. There was only one way out of his dilemma, and that was to deliver the telegram to 7 Fortune Row in the same way as they were planning to do the others, but this time on his own. Jay could neither bring himself to tell Vince of its existence, nor open it himself as he had done the others.

He went across to the window and peered out at the trees, his mind obsessed by the problem of his father's telegram. It was dark, and the sky was overcast with rain clouds, but he did not switch on the light. He knew he ought not to withhold the telegram, yet how could he engineer its appearance without himself being suspect? The side of him that calculated the risks, and measured his own capacities against those of adults, knew that the wisest course was to remain in ignorance of the contents of the telegram. That way he would be genuinely surprised at its message; that way he need have no fear of his grandmother's knack of detecting pretence.

CHAPTER SIX

FOILED

Jay hurried back with the bread and the bag of potatoes, hoping that his grandmother wouldn't think up any further errands, for he had arranged to meet Vince at the tree. If no-one was around, they could make sure *The Henty* was safe and move her to some better hiding-place up-stream. There were bound to be workmen some time or other to deal with the tree, sightseers too, and *The Henty* was too near at hand for safety, and for their own peace of mind.

He stood in the kitchen still clutching the bag of potatoes.

"You're going out." His grandmother was merely stating what she knew was his intention. Jay wondered what could be done to prevent her knowing your intentions, how you could make her understand that you didn't always want to say what you were going to do. Then he smiled to himself. She knew nothing of those expeditions, those perilous excursions across the roof, nor did she know about *The Henty*.

"Vince hasn't seen the tree yet," he explained; "I'm going to meet him there."

"You'll put your boots on this time."

"O.K."

"With last night's rain it'll be every bit as bad as yesterday morning."

For a moment he watched her placing everything ready for cooking—flour, sultanas, lard, cocoa. It would be good if he could have something to take with them.

"There's some flapjack left in the tin; you can finish that up," she said. "But don't be late."

"Thanks, Gran." He took the red tin down from the shelf.

"And don't make a lot of noise going out."

"O.K." He delved into the tin, remembering that his father was asleep upstairs. Three pieces left. Pity there weren't four.

"There's a bag in the drawer. It's only half past nine, you know. You don't have to stay out all the morning looking at one tree."

"No, but it's a pretty big tree."

"Go on. Off with you," she ordered.

The sun was breaking through; it promised to be a good morning. They must make sure *The Henty* was safe. In the holidays it had been easy to time their outings; with all day, every day at their disposal, a few minutes lost were of little account and they could afford to wait till any intruders made off. But now time was limited and every opportunity to be in *The Henty* was important.

Jay wrapped the flapjacks. "I'll get my boots. 'Bye, Gran." He went out to the shed, where the wellington boots were lined up on the lower shelf. The shed had a warm, woody smell; there was sawdust on the floor. Jay decided to leave his shoes there and not go back indoors with them; so pushing the packet for their lunch in his anorak pocket he made his way through the side passage to Fortune Row.

Vince was already there. "Saw you go in," he shouted.

"Come on," ordered Jay, impatient to reach *The Henty*. As soon as they came in sight of the tree, their hopes of getting away in *The Henty* were dashed. They were not alone by the river, not a bit of it. There was Mr Joiner from next door, selecting suitable sticks for his plants; there was Stan Richards loitering around as though he had just plucked up enough interest to favour the fallen tree with his presence; there was the photographer from the Anderbury Press; and finally four children in high spirits were clambering over the huge trunk. Vince and Jay came alongside.

"Crumbs," said Vince, surveying the tree. "Wish I'd seen it come down. Bang. Crash."

Jay saw that, where the roots had been wrenched from the earth, the swollen river had now extended its reach, making a fresh inlet. Stan came up, examined the roots and the encroaching river, then sloped off with his hands in his pockets, ignoring Jay and Vince.

The photographer asked the children to stand by the tree.

"Hey, mister, he found it first." Vince pointed at Jay. Stan turned round at the sound of Vince's voice, then continued on his way.

"We'll be in it," offered Vince, mimicking, pretending he was operating a camera, but the photographer was not inclined to take suggestions from others. Neither had Vince any intention of being refused; he disappeared in the hollow trunk. Jay laughed, guessing that at the crucial moment Vince would pop up his head.

"All right, you kids. Have it your own way."

"I saw it struck, sir. Honest I did," declared Jay.

"Well, stand by if you must, but don't be fool enough to stick your head up at the wrong moment."

"What we going to do?" asked Vince once the photographer had gone.

"Dunno. Could go on to the bridge for a bit. We can see *The Henty* then, and the others might be gone when we come back." Jay eyed Mr Joiner and the children.

"You're joking," said Vince. Didn't they know Mr Joiner and the hours he spent in his garden over the minutest jobs! He'd be all day by the tree, choosing sticks, trimming them to his requirements.

"We could do one of the telegrams," suggested Vince. Jay was loth to go indoors again to fetch them, but he could remember the addresses. "We'll go and snoop out some of the places," he agreed.

"O.K." Vince leapt ahead whistling. It would never do to betray their interest in what was concealed beneath the bridge.

"I got something," called Jay, whisking the package from his pocket.

Vince waited for him. "Let's go and sit on the bridge and eat them."

"O.K." Jay caught up with him. "We'll find those addresses afterwards."

They shared the flapjacks before they reached the bridge.

"Guess this's O.K.," observed Vince, peering through the willow-herb.

"They'll see you, you nut," said Jay angrily.

"Won't," denied Vince.

"Bet you don't remember those addresses." Jay leant over the bridge.

"Bet I do."

"You tell me then."

"Tell you nothin'." Vince concentrated on enjoying the flapjack, conscious that beneath them on the shadowy water *The Henty* was hidden.

"Eleven Oxen Lane. Two The Slattery," boasted Jay, "and I know all the others."

"So what."

CHAPTER SEVEN

ANOTHER MESSAGE

Jay hung around in Fortune Row for Vince. Since he was the organist Mr Lewis left for church early, and Jay, preferring to be independent, did not wait for his grandmother. The church in Hovant was small; Hovant had never expanded as Lisham and Anderbury had done, despite the extension of the railway.

Vince emerged from number ten. "You got it?" he signalled, and for answer Jay tapped his pocket. "You bet."

It was warm and humid, and much of Hovant was still asleep. Vince thought of the river and *The Henty*. It would have been easy this morning to rescue the boat from her nearness to prying eyes and the scene of the fallen tree, and for his own part he would willingly have turned off at the end of Fortune Row and made his way to the path by the river. But that was one thing Jay wouldn't do, of that he was sure; Jay wouldn't stay away from church. Perhaps it was different for Jay; his father and his grandmother were at church, so they'd know if Jay didn't turn up. But then Vince knew it was rather more than that that drew Jay to the church.

Vince nudged Jay as they went into the small church, and Jay grinned at the sight of Mr Barnard sitting at the front with two small boys. Mr Barnard had sparse brown hair, Mr Barnard wore horn-rimmed spectacles, Mr Barnard played the guitar, Mr Barnard also played cricket; but Mr Barnard knew nothing of the secret message in Jay's pocket.

"Hallo, Jay," greeted Mr Barnard.

"Hallo." Jay smiled secretly at Vince.

"Hallo, Vince. Nice to see you."

"Hallo, Mr Barnard." Vince sat down beside Jay, conveying dramatic messages with his dark eyes. The organ sounded, and it was easy to whisper under cover of its vibrant notes, though Jay knew his father would detect their voices. People were coming into the service, more children, Jay's grandmother.

It was the hymn before they went to their classes. Jay held his book, waiting for the organ, when Vince pointed to the third verse. Jay followed the direction of his finger—'We've a message to give . . .' Vince winked boldly and pretended to drop a letter through an imaginary letter-box.

Mr Barnard, surveying his handful of boys, caught Jay's eye. Jay reddened, not from any shame at the private game he and Vince were playing at that moment, but from the knowledge that he had read a private message to Mr Barnard; that unknown to Mr Barnard, that message was in his pocket. It wasn't right; but then, he argued, that wasn't his fault. On Friday night he hadn't minded too much about that side of things, but since then the possession of Mr Barnard's telegram was having a strange effect on him. Before, he was pleased with himself, sure of his plans; now he was beginning to feel disturbed, unsure. Brushing aside the unwelcome thoughts, he joined in the rousing tune, hardly aware of the meaning of the words till they came to the third verse, and those words he could not ignore.

> We've a message to give to the nations,
> That the Lord who reigneth above
> Has sent us His Son to save us,
> And show us that God is love.

Vince, still mimicking a postman, appeared to find the hymn amusing. In the press of leaving the church to go to their classroom, Jay managed to shake off the feeling that the hymn had something to say to him. All through the lesson his mind wandered to *The Henty*, to the expedition he and Vince had planned for later on, to the fallen tree.

They were away before Mr Barnard had a chance to speak to them, running through the path at the back of the church, up the hill to East Side Lane where Mr and Mrs Barnard lived with their three children.

"Bet old Barney 'ud never guess it was us." Vince was pleased with himself.

They slackened their pace as they approached the end of his road, for, though every detail had been planned most carefully, they needed to rehearse the actions once more. From the slight eminence where they stood, they could look down on Hovant, and also view the length of East Side Lane. It was a sleepy road at the best of times, so they reckoned that on a Sunday morning there was a good chance that not a soul would be around. It proved to be just as they hoped—no sign of life, not even a dog or a cat to be seen. Nine was in the middle of the houses on the righthand side, a small house with a yellow front door.

Vince produced a handkerchief. "Remove all fingerprints. Bet you never thought of that."

"Did," contradicted Jay. "What about the other fingerprints anyway?"

"They won't still be there," argued Vince, "but we got to shift ours. Here, let's have it." He waited while Jay took the envelope from his blazer pocket.

The silent house with its gaily painted door, and the soiled orange envelope in their hands, presented a challenge, and Jay argued that they would only be doing what should have been done a year ago. He knew that Vince hankered after being postman, and the conflicting thoughts in his own mind made it easier for him to surrender this privilege and merely act as watchman.

Vince breathed on the envelope and then rubbed it carefully between the folds of his clean handkerchief. "That's about done it," he grinned; "all traces removed."

"Go on. Now," ordered Jay, "or he'll be coming. If you see me buzz off, you must go on as if you were walking down the road. If I'm still here, it's O.K. for you to drop it in."

"Here goes." Vince swaggered along the unmade road, one hand in his pocket, the other slipped inside his blazer, holding the telegram between the folds of the handkerchief. Jay watched him walk the whole length of the road, then return slowly till he was outside number nine. This was it. Vince was out of sight for a brief moment. Jay felt his heart racing. There was no turning back now; it was done, the message was delivered. But where was Vince? He couldn't have been caught; the Barnards had all been at church. No, it was all right. There was Vince, sauntering back, pretending it had been as simple as anything, that he hadn't turned a hair. Now they had to get back to Fortune Row without meeting up with Mr Barnard.

Vince was grinning triumphantly. "Piece of cake," he said. "Let's go and see *The Henty*."

Jay hesitated, knowing that he would be expected home, knowing too that once you were tempted to get into *The Henty* you didn't want to leave her. That was the thing with the river and *The Henty*—you just couldn't get away. It was a thing he liked; it made *The Henty*.

"I've got to get home. There'll be a row if I'm late for dinner, but we can just have a look at her." Then his mind was back with the telegrams. There was one great disappointment in it—the fact that he and Vince would be excluded from the surprise it gave; they might never hear anything more about Mr Barnard's telegram, and that would be most unsatisfactory. He'd know with the one for his father; that was different.

They reached Fortune Row and ambled through the spare ground by Stan Richards' house.

"Wonder if old Barney's home yet," said Vince. They laughed, close in the knowledge of their plans. As they came out by the river path, they saw Stan and a friend by the gate in the back fence. Stan had the fishing rod that was Vince's envy, and his friend was bending down, sorting out some tackle.

"Blow," muttered Vince. You never felt so free with people like Stan around. And certainly they couldn't go to *The Henty*. He could imagine the sort of remarks Stan would make about the boat—'That old tub.' Stan with his new motor-bike, and his fishing gear.

Vince signalled to Jay behind him that it was useless continuing by the river, then he pranced along, swinging an imaginary fishing line.

They were back in Fortune Row.

"See you," said Jay, opening the gate of number seven.

Vince began to whistle.

"If me and my dad go out this afternoon, I'll call for you," offered Jay. " 'Bout half past two."

"Yeh," accepted Vince. He was hoping there might be some such invitation. It was good fun going with Mr Lewis—the woods, the track by the railway. "Wonder what old Barney's thinking." It was exciting having inside information. Vince went on his way whistling.

CHAPTER EIGHT

CONVERSATION PIECE

Jay came into the kitchen swinging his satchel. From the window he could see his grandmother taking the washing from the line. Her guess that the summer was over was wrong; the September day had been fine and warm, so warm that she had left the windows wide open. It was the sort of day that made him long for the freedom of the river, for *The Henty* that had made the summer holidays for him and Vince. You could do things in a boat.

Today, early for school, they had an opportunity of delivering another of the telegrams. Knowing that the only chance they had of going to Lisham, without making a special journey, was at school time, they had made an effort to catch the early bus. But the envelope was still in Jay's pocket, for when they reached the address a large furniture van was outside —the occupants were moving.

Mr Lewis came from the garden shed holding a piece of timber. His grandmother was still reaching up, unpegging clothes.

"You know what I heard," she said to him. "I met Mrs Barnard."

Jay saw the shopping basket on the table, with bread, bananas, a bottle of orange squash.

"Most peculiar. Telegram." Her speech was punctuated like the stops in the telegrams, as she retrieved each garment from the line.

Jay gasped, half afraid, and yet he could have laughed with excitement. They were going to know after all; he'd have something to tell Vince. That was the way he liked things—having news to impart.

"Mm. A telegram. And a year late. There it was when they got home from church."

The breeze was moving the rambler rose. His father was no longer considering the wood in his hand but was looking at Jay's grandmother, his interest roused by her story.

"Bit the worse for wear," she continued.

"Was it important? Has he any clue as to why it was delayed?"

"You know, Mrs Barnard said it was an answer to prayer. Not its being held up."

Jay leant against the cupboard, close to the window. Outside, everything was colourful and clean, but somehow Jay felt guilty.

"You remember Mr Barnard's young brother went to New Zealand without telling them?"

"Yes. Nice young fellow. Mad on boats."

"They never got over him not telling them about the New Zealand business." She folded the clothes into the waiting basket.

"No, I suppose not."

"And when his plane crashed it left them upset, not knowing things. This was his telegram telling them he was going, and all the news to follow."

"But of course he was killed, so they never heard," said Mr Lewis.

"Still they feel better about it now."

Jay felt better about it too. He was glad it was that sort of a message. Though they played Mr

Barnard up at times, he was a sport. In fact they'd done him a good turn. He and Vince had been pretty smart. As soon as they got out to *The Henty* tonight he'd tell Vince. He dashed into the garden, full of the thought of the evening's secret venture, and of the outcome of their venture yesterday.

"Hallo, Dad."

"Hallo, son. Had a good day?"

"Rotten. Dad, do I have to do——"

"You're not old enough to decide what you do or you don't do at school." Mrs Lewis pocketed the clothes pegs. "I wish I'd had half your chances."

Jay sighed. Then he saw his father's eyes twinkle. "What would you have been, Gran?" he asked.

"What would I have been? I'd have—well, never mind. We'll have some tea. It's no good grieving."

The evening was still, as though waiting for something to happen; neither was there any sound from downstairs, but then Jay remembered his grandmother saying she had some letters to write, and that hardly entailed any noise. Darkness was coming earlier now, making both journeys hazardous, yet there was something doubly inviting about a journey in the dark, something attractive about the spice of risk and danger. Tonight, he and Vince were going to shift *The Henty*, release her from her present anchorage to the stretch that few people frequented, the backwater with its overhanging branches and stagnant water.

Jay made sure his torch was safely in his pocket. Vince had promised to bring the Pifco hand lamp that he had for Christmas. Closing the window behind him, Jay edged his way down the sloping roof, placing his feet sideways to prevent himself slithering on the smooth slates. Vince was signalling with his lamp, and it occurred to Jay that this was something they could do when it was no longer possible to get out in *The Henty*.

Until they reached the fallen tree they had no need of any light, for every inch of the way was familiar. Now Vince switched on the lamp and held it in the hollow trunk. "You want one of these." He proudly surveyed the powerful beams that searched out the rottenness of the tree. "How we going to find out who put those telegrams there?"

"When we've delivered them all, someone'll create a thundering row, you bet they will." Jay too, wanted the culprit unmasked; but for both of them the most urgent matter at the moment was the safety of *The Henty*. Past the tree Jay flickered his torch through the weeds on the bank, then stooped down to feel for the rope that held *The Henty* from drifting.

"She's O.K," he whispered.

They crept to the edge of the Ander. There was hardly any movement on the water; no breeze rippled the surface. Vince untied the rope, then drew *The Henty* to the bank so that Jay could board her. Jay held on to the side; the very feel of the boat was exhilarating. The sound of the water as *The Henty* took his weight, the awareness of Vince crouched on the bank roused his anticipation. With their home-made paddle, Jay held the boat against the bank, while Vince joined him; then paddling gently into mid-stream, he guided her beneath the arch of the bridge. Vince switched on his lamp once more, his dark eyes lit with its brightness.

"Yours is too bright. Have my torch," whispered Jay. *The Henty* responded to every stroke. If only they had some decent oars! He imagined their impact on the water, the powerful strokes forcing *The Henty* along.

"I'm starving," declared Vince.

"Shut up," said Jay; "we haven't got anything. Here. I'll tell you about old Barney."

"You heard?" Vince made the boat lurch in his excitement. His recent hunger was forgotten.

"Stow it, you nut; you'll upset us," reproved Jay.

"She wouldn't upset."

"Well, I heard my gran telling Dad. It was this brother of his."

"Whose brother?"

"Barney's of course."

Vince listened to the story, then whistled softly, remembering the words of the telegram. *The Henty* glided ahead. "Guess he never got to New Zealand, or the plane could've crashed when it landed."

They let *The Henty* drift, thinking of Mr Barnard's brother.

Vince shifted his feet. "If we hadn't delivered it, he wouldn't have known. Reckon that's one up for us. He got the message."

Jay moved his hand round the paddle, dipping the blade into the dark stream. The message. There was the word again. The hymn. 'Sent us His Son to save us, and shew us that God is love.' He knew all about it, that it was important, the most important thing of all, but just now he didn't want to think about it. He also pushed aside the picture of his grandmother in the garden, reaching for the white pillowcases and saying it was an answer to prayer. Suppose the tree hadn't been struck by lightning, then those telegrams would still be in the hollow trunk and Mr Barnard's prayer would have been unanswered. But the storm was God's doing—so . . . It was too difficult to work out. His father prayed about things, about knowing the right thing to do, but for himself he had never felt the need of this; he just liked going his own way, at least for the present.

It was eerie in the backwater. The branches of the trees on the banks met across the stream, closing them in. They felt trapped and scared in the darkness. Vince turned on the hand lamp, searching out the place where they had decided to berth *The Henty*. While its light re-assured them to a certain extent, it also made startling shadows, it created odd shapes like jungle creatures lurking on the bank. In the daytime everything looked so different, though even then the backwater had a desolate air.

"Take her in." Vince directed the beam to the willow tree and Jay manoeuvred the boat as best he could.

"When I get her alongside, you nip out," he ordered Vince. "Don't take the lamp; leave that in the boat."

Vince was loth to relinquish the lamp.

"You take the torch then," offered Jay.

They touched the shore; there was the sound of the water lapping against the bank, the feel of its strength against *The Henty*.

"We can get out here and pull her along under the tree afterwards," suggested Vince.

The drooping willow branches looked forbidding.

Vince scrambled ashore, then held *The Henty* while Jay followed.

"Bet she'll be O.K. here." Vince directed the lamp to reveal where they intended tying up the boat. Once this was achieved neither of them wanted to stay. Nothing about the backwater drew them, and they started home, creeping along the edge of the water with Jay's torch for guide, till they reached the main river path. Now they felt free, released from the sense of being shut in. No longer in need of the torch, they moved confidently ahead to the bridge. Hovant was asleep, most of it anyway, and the thought made them more daring, when suddenly Jay stood stock-still.

"Look," he whispered.

There was someone ahead, near the tree, with a light. For a moment it disappeared from view, then they saw it once more.

"What we going to do?" Vince was worried. Jay too, was thinking of the problem of getting back home without being observed.

"Wait, I s'pose," he answered. They had already been out some time, but they daren't risk going on when an unknown person was in their path. Whoever it was was bound to spell trouble.

"He could be ages," Vince whispered.

Jay took a step forward. "He won't see us yet."

"Might be she." Vince's laugh was rather shaky.

"Come on," encouraged Jay; "we've got to scare him off."

" 'Course." Vince felt better at the suggestion. "How?"

"We'll get on the bridge, then throw something in the river. He'll hear it." Jay was standing by the bridge. Not far ahead a torch was moving by the fallen tree.

"P'raps it's Mr Joiner getting some more sticks. You won't scare him off."

They were on the bridge, groping for pebbles.

"Tell you what," said Jay. He stood up and peered over to the water beneath. "I'll throw mine first, while you keep watch at the end. No-one'll see you in the weeds there, and you'll be able to tell whether he puts his torch out directly he hears the splash. If he does that'll mean he's scared; if he doesn't, we'll have to wait. I shall duck directly I've thrown it, just in case he sees me. He'll be able to tell the direction of the sound, so he's bound to look this way."

"O.K." Vince moved to the shelter of the water-side growth and waited and watched. The torch was still evident in the region of the tree, a blob of light moving in the darkness.

The impact of the stone on the water sounded clear through the night. Unshaken by the sudden disturbance of the quiet, Vince gave no sign of his presence, but the holder of the torch extinguished the small light immediately. Jay crept alongside, feeling the roughness of the bridge, but neither spoke—only waited to see if the night prowler made any move.

"Shall I throw mine?" asked Vince at last.

"Yeh." Jay strained to see if he could make out any figure.

Vince stood up, his back to the bridge. Clad in a dark jersey and jeans, there was little chance of his being detected. With a quick thrust of his arm he hurtled the stone through the air. They heard it drop into the water, then all was quiet, too quiet.

"S'pose he's waiting for us." Vince was scared, but another fear was urging them on, the fear that their long absence might be discovered.

"We got to go," decided Jay.

CHAPTER NINE

MESSAGE GIVEN

Jay shivered, calculating the best thing to do in the darkness. Though they had met no-one between the bridge and Vince's garden, and had felt their way over the tree trunk rather than betray their presence by using the torch, Jay could not shake off the feeling that the snooper had them in view.

Vince was safe in his own room, and Jay had now to traverse the bridge, the narrow, creaky bridge between nine and eight Fortune Row. It was dark, and he was tired. Anything to be in bed, anything not to have to cross that narrow strip of wood in the darkness. Then he felt angry with himself. He could do it easily, of course he could. Who said he couldn't. He felt for the torch in his pocket, just to be sure of his first foothold. But the torch had gone. It must be there; he couldn't have dropped it. There was no torch in his pockets. Vince, perhaps Vince had it. No, he remembered taking it from him. He'd have to go back early in the morning, before anyone else found it. There was nothing else he could do.

Worried, he edged his way onto the roof of number eight, and then it was that he noticed the light in his grandmother's bedroom, a rosy pink glow shining through the curtains.

Jay kept quite still, crouching at the edge of the roof. It must be almost midnight, for, though his grandmother insisted on his going to bed early, she herself rarely turned in much before twelve. So what was he to do now? What could he do but wait? Her room was next to his and she would detect any movement on the roof, and if his window squeaked she would know something was up. And suppose by some chance she had gone into his room and discovered his absence, and was waiting for his return! He waited, cold and uncomfortable.

The light was extinguished, there was no warm glow from her window. In the whole of Fortune Row he could see no light shining. Still he waited. His grandmother declared she was asleep as soon as her head touched the pillow, but how could he be sure? It wasn't worth risking discovery when he was so nearly home. It seemed an age that he waited before making his way over the slates to his own window. The sash slipped open without a creak and he climbed into his room. Safe at last, he felt pleased with himself. Tomorrow he'd tell Vince about the light, about having to wait till his grandmother was asleep. But of course, now was the time, the time to deliver that other telegram. Everything was perfect. Give Gran a bit longer to be well and truly off, and he'd snoop downstairs and put it on the mat. As long as he could manage to get it from the drawer quietly. The key turned soundlessly, everything responded to his touch, and the telegram he wanted was not in the rubber band with the others, but lying by itself. Now for it. He grasped the door handle, turning it slowly, not letting it jerk back.

The landing was dark, darker than his room somehow, and he was sure he could hear his grandmother snoring. Not that she would ever admit to snoring. Now for the fifteen stairs—three, then two at the bend, then straight down and almost directly ahead the doormat.

The tune was going through his mind again, a line for each stair. 'We've a message to give, That the Lord who reigneth above'. He wasn't doing anything wrong, of course he wasn't. 'Has sent us His Son to save us'. He'd been thinking about that by the river. It wasn't as if he was saying no to God; there was plenty of time, next year. He put his hand on the doormat, prickly coconut matting. Everything was still in Fortune Row; not a soul dreamt what was going on, not even Vince. Now he placed the envelope where he judged it would fall if pushed through the letter-box, a little sideways to look more realistic. It was done. He turned to retrace his steps, preparing to count the stairs so that there was no danger of his stumbling.

There was a thin line of light showing beneath the kitchen door. She wasn't in bed! Why hadn't he noticed the light when he came down? If only he hadn't kept to the wall he might have seen it! A movement in the kitchen, and in a sudden panic Jay hurried up the stairs and pulled off his jersey and jeans. He might have known it wasn't twelve; they hadn't been out all that time. He hastily got into his pyjamas then stood by the closed door, listening. She was stoking the boiler for the night, raking out the ashes. He slipped into bed, his heart pounding. Now she was coming into the hall, locking the kitchen door behind her. He listened, but not a sound reached him. Had she seen it? She couldn't help seeing it, unless she came up to bed without switching on the light.

Jay sat up, then leant over towards the door. A faint glimmer of light came from the landing outside. She had turned on the light, so she couldn't miss the envelope. Still everything downstairs was quiet; then he heard the bolt of the front door pushed into position, the safety chain linked; small sounds, that normally never reached him, now filled him with apprehension. He counted the stairs as she mounted, for he was aware even of the tread of her slippered feet. Now she was in her room. And the telegram? The minutes dragged by as he wondered whether she had opened it. Tomorrow his father would see it. He heard the small click of the switch of her bedside lamp. Would she be asleep as soon as her head touched the pillow, or was there something that disturbed her in the telegram? But Jay could not sleep.

CHAPTER TEN

THE YEAR BETWEEN

"Jay!"

He started up to find his grandmother shaking him by the shoulders.

"Now that's the last of your reading in bed." She pointed angrily at the book on the chair by the bedside, the book whose pages he had been idly turning merely to fill the interval between coming upstairs and starting out for *The Henty*.

Then he remembered the telegram, and he looked away. Mrs Lewis picked up the book, and closed it with a snap before pulling back the curtains and going downstairs.

Jay tried to hurry, but tiredness hampered all his efforts at speed. It seemed as though he'd only had a few minutes sleep; it couldn't have been more, not by the way he felt, and he didn't fancy breakfast. He crept guiltily into the kitchen and sat down at the table.

"Hallo, son." Mr Lewis was already eating egg and bacon.

Mrs Lewis regarded Jay severely, then went across to the cooker, while Jay made a valiant effort to appear carefree.

Mr Lewis rubbed his chin thoughtfully. "Gran tells me you were reading late last night."

Jay grinned sheepishly.

"Must have been something good to keep you at it so long." He knew how rarely Jay settled at anything.

Jay thought furiously. What was it he was reading? For the life of him he couldn't remember. "Oh, nothing much, Dad. I didn't read an awful long time." He consoled himself that at least that was the truth. Then he noticed the telegram beside his father's plate. Yes, what he said might be all right; it was all the other things that were the trouble—going to *The Henty*, getting delayed by the prowler, losing his torch, putting the telegram on the mat, finding his grandmother was in the kitchen when he thought she was safely in bed. Those things kept going round and round in his mind.

Mr Lewis saw Jay's glance transfixed by the telegram. "So you didn't hear this come in the door?" he said.

Jay blinked. "Telegram," he stammered, and there was nothing counterfeit about his confusion; indeed he was far more alarmed than if its arrival had been unexpected.

"It's all right," assured his grandmother, placing the bowl of porridge in front of him. "Nothing for you to worry about. Except that if you don't get a move on you're going to be late for school."

School! He felt too utterly weary and worried to face school, though it would provide an escape from any questions. "Yes, Gran," he answered meekly, and took a drink of tea. Surprisingly he felt better. "What does it say?"

Mr Lewis picked up the telegram. "It says, 'Accept offer. Collect tomorrow Saturday by 10 a.m. Packer'."

Jay blew on the spoonful of porridge. It didn't sound a terribly important message. Something to do with railway tickets. "Collect tomorrow, Saturday," he repeated.

"Well, Jay, if you were even half awake, you'd realise tomorrow isn't Saturday; it's Wednesday."

"Oh." He supposed he ought to laugh at his own stupidity, but it wasn't easy pretending to be amused, and anyway he didn't feel like laughing.

"You'll go to bed early tonight," warned Mrs Lewis.

"The whole point of this telegram is that it's late," said Mr Lewis.

"Oh."

"A year late."

Jay knew he ought to register more surprise, but he just continued to stare at the telegram. His head was going round; the porridge was most unappetising.

"Yes, I was after some items to complete the London, Brighton and South Coast Railway collection, a few items that would probably have doubled the value of what I had. Mr Packer was selling out, and there were a good few buyers after his collection. He gave me first option on those particular items. I made an offer. This was to tell me he accepted my offer so long as I fetched them on the Saturday. He was going abroad."

"Didn't you get them?" gasped Jay.

"No. As you see, the telegram was delayed."

"You mean someone else's got them?"

"That's about it."

Jay was really awake now, awake with anger.

"But Dad, that's not fair, that's——" He nearly choked over the porridge.

"Get your breakfast down you, and stop talking," ordered his grandmother. Then she sighed. "Yes, that would have got your father a tidy sum, if he'd had those extra items. I can remember the old London, Brighton and South Coast."

"But Dad, can't you do something? Can't you get someone for it?"

Jay could not contain his fury. This was different from Mr Barnard's message. His was put right. But this could never be put right.

"Don't know about that, Jay."

Jay couldn't understand his father's calm attitude. "They're yours," he declared; "they ought to pay."

"That would mean finding out who slipped this through the letter-box last night, who was around between eleven and midnight. It wasn't there when Gran went upstairs to put the hot-water bottle in her bed."

So that was what she was doing.

"Well, maybe I'd better not swear to that," she intervened.

Jay felt the red creep up his face. How nearly he'd been caught! The thought of it made him even more angry, angry at the real culprit, angry at his father's attitude, angry at his grandmother for so nearly trapping him. "You can't just do nothing," he declared before he realised that any investigation would entail his own discovery.

"I know it was a bit like a chance of a lifetime to get hold of those items. But someone else has them now, and that's it as far as I'm concerned."

"That's rotten," snapped Jay.

"I know. I felt bad about it when I read this a little while ago. Now I'm wondering what message it has for me now. God knows about it."

Message. Message. He didn't want to hear anything more about messages. "It was meant to reach you ages ago. Why didn't God let it reach you then?" he demanded.

Mr Lewis looked at Jay, wondering why he had taken the matter so much to heart. "That's what we may discover. Mr Barnard had a telegram too. Did your grandmother tell you?"

"No." He looked down at his porridge, knowing he was in a rotten temper.

"Quite an interesting mystery brewing in Hovant," said Mr Lewis, surprised at Jay's lack of response to the odd goings on.

"Jay if you don't hurry up——"

"Yes, Gran." He felt queer again, horribly tired and horribly frightened. "I think I've got a headache, or——" He pushed the plate away. Now she'd ask questions, take his temperature. And Vince would be in a flap. But it was no good, his head was swimming.

"Up you go."

Her order was more than welcome. He crept back to his room, and, like her, as soon as his head touched the pillow, sleep came.

CHAPTER ELEVEN

MESSRS BARNARD AND LEWIS

Jay locked and unlocked the small drawer that contained the remainder of the telegrams, unsure what to do about them, arguing with himself that he was not the one to blame for their non-delivery, and what was a few days compared with a whole year. And yet he knew that he had started something that had now got out of hand. He and Vince had planned the whole thing; now it was going its way. It had led to things he hadn't intended, it had led to deceiving his father. He was no longer sure that he wanted to deliver the rest of the envelopes. He and Vince had tampered with them, and in some cases this was obvious, and Jay was dreading the outcome. Despite all his arguments, he could no longer quieten his conscience, or shake off the sense of shame at pretending to his father and grandmother. Things weren't the same at home. It wasn't that he was afraid of his father; it was himself he was afraid of—afraid of what he might do or say. And there was only one solution—own up to the whole thing. In a few minutes it would be time for club. Vince was probably waiting outside.

As if in answer to his thoughts he heard his grandmother's voice. "Jay."

"Coming." He ran downstairs.

"Now come straight home," she cautioned.

"O.K. I'm all right." He didn't want a fuss. Tuesday's day in bed was something of the past, and he didn't want it dragged up to curtail his freedom.

"You didn't see yourself Tuesday morning, my boy. Half asleep."

Jay escaped into Fortune Row. "Hey, Vince," he yelled.

To tell Vince of the telegram at number seven would share his own concern about the whole matter. It would also impress Vince, and Jay liked the sensation. His spirits rose at the prospect of relating how near he had been to discovery, how much the real culprit was to blame for denying his father that special opportunity.

"We got a telegram." He walked ahead, waiting for Vince's reaction.

"You never." You could rouse Vince's interest easily. Vince caught up with Jay. Then his expression changed. "Oh, you mean a proper one. That's different."

"It wasn't. It was one of them."

"It couldn't've been." Vince was annoyed now.

"Who said." Jay laughed at Vince's fury. "This one was addressed to my dad, so I wasn't going to leave it with the others."

Vince was about to retaliate.

"Well you wouldn't want someone opening your dad's telegram." Jay's words condemned them both.

"S'pose not." Vince's good humour returned.

"Anyway I never opened it."

"What did it say?"

They ambled towards the church, while Jay described his night adventures, his near escape, the morning after and the message in the telegram.

"What's your dad going to do?"

"Nothing." Jay kicked a stone angrily.

"Bet my dad would. He'd kick up a shindy."

"Shut up," snapped Jay.

They were late for club, and Mr Barnard was already organising the small group of boys. John Phillips and Peter Jackman were thirteen; the others, Tony, Ian and Alec, were twelve like Jay and Vince.

"Hallo, Jay," greeted Mr Barnard. "Come on, Vince. You're just in time for our experiment."

Jay saw the telegram on the table beside Mr Barnard's Bible, a hand lamp and two torches, all uncomfortable reminders of his own activities. With a shock he realised that he had not retrieved his own torch. Suppose someone else had found it. In any case it would probably be spoilt. There was his name on it, on a small slip of paper with 'J. Lewis', secured by a piece of sellotape on top.

They pulled their chairs up to the table, scraping the legs noisily on the wooden floor of the hall, not over-concerned with anyone but themselves. Then Mr Barnard began to tell them the story of his unusual telegram. It was passed from hand to hand, but neither Jay nor Vince betrayed the fact that their eyes had scanned its message before. The rest of the boys insisted on knowing what Mr Barnard was going to do, storming him with their suggestions.

The temptation to carve for himself an important place in the evening was too great for Jay, even against the risks it might hold.

"We've had one as well, sir."

"You've had one?" Now they all turned to Jay. "When was that?" asked Mr Barnard. It was not the first time Jay and Vince had managed to distract attention from what he was trying to say.

"Well, it was there Tuesday morning."

"Tuesday, eh?"

"I mean my gran found it on the mat, same as you did, sir. She found it when she was going up to bed."

"What time was that?" asked Mr Barnard.

"Middle of the night, sir," laughed Jay.

"So we have a night messenger. Works in the dark," said Mr Barnard.

Jay almost stole the show. The boys were wanting to know about his telegram.

"What's it say?" asked Tony.

"Now that," interrupted Mr Barnard, "is not our business. We can ask Mr Lewis for that bit of information if we want it."

Jay was nettled; his temper rose. He'd intended telling the whole story, getting them angry about the raw deal his father had had. But he was ashamed too, for, by his words, Mr Barnard had condemned what he and Vince had done.

"Now there's several things we're going to do this evening." Mr Barnard tried to recapture their wandering thoughts. He knew Jay's natural ability to divert others, an ability he occasionally used to help matters on Thursdays but at other times used to hinder the work.

"We're going to invent our own code of signalling with lights. Let's see which group can come up with the most efficient method."

"Beat yer hands down." Vince looked across at Tony and Alec.

"We'll go on with the semaphore," continued Mr Barnard. "Peter's quite a hand at that now."

Peter began demonstrating the alphabet.

"That's jammy," snubbed Vince.

"You mean that's all you can do," retorted Peter.

"That's enough, you lads," reproved Mr Barnard. "When we've worked out our code we'll pick out some messages God had sent to us, and do some transmitting. After that we'll go in the kitchen for some eats."

"Whooppee," shouted Tony and Vince.

"What we got?" asked Alec.

Mr Barnard ignored the question. "While we're having our refreshments we'll see if we can engage on a bit of detection work."

"You mean us, sir?" asked Vince innocently.

"Who else, you idiot," Peter chimed in.

"Can't we do that now?" suggested Alec.

"You just have to go to the post office, and let them find out." Ian was critical.

"They wouldn't tell you anything, you nut," argued Alec; "they'd keep it to themselves."

Jay had been watching the others carefully, feeling superior with his inside information. "That's right, sir; they never tell you anything. Anyway we—we want to know."

"That's about it, Jay. We want to know. The post office could tell us a great deal. I was going to send a letter off this evening, but perhaps Mr Lewis and I could work together over it. Mind you, the post office won't know who the secret agent was who slipped them in our letter-boxes. So I'm looking forward to your bright ideas about that. Between us we ought to uncover something by next week."

Vince was enjoying the whole thing, but now Jay

began to feel disturbed. Where was this detective lark going to lead? Any other time and object, and he would have pitted his wits against the other boys, clamoured for his own ideas. But now there was a barrier between him and them, a worse barrier between him and Mr Barnard. He tried to dismiss his feelings and concentrate on practising semaphore. They divided into two groups under Peter and John, to work out a scheme of transmitting with flashes. They argued noisily, but Jay let Vince do all the talking; he couldn't concentrate on making a code.

"Here is the message."

Jay turned at the sound of Mr Barnard's voice clear above the hubbub in the hall. It had startled him, and his heart began to race. Mr Barnard was holding a Bible in his hands. Jay shook himself. Silly of him to be taken unawares. It was just what Mr Barnard had said they were going to do, look out some messages from God. Messages! He couldn't shake off the importance of the word.

Mr Barnard went on reading. "Here is the message we heard from him and pass on to you: that God is light, and in him there is no darkness at all. If we claim to be sharing in his life while we walk in the dark, our words and our lives are a lie."

Jay's eyes were riveted on the Bible in Mr Barnard's hand; his mind was caught by the message. 'God is light . . . our words and our lives are a lie.' He knew it was true; it was what was happening at this very moment. His words and his actions were lies. He and Vince weren't really helping to discover the truth; they were, in fact, trying to cover it up. He might contribute some clever scheme, and he prided himself he could think up something better than the others, but his plan would be aimed at concealing part of the truth.

"But if we walk in the light . . ." Jay tried not to listen, hoping Mr Barnard would put the book down. "—we are being cleansed from every sin by the blood of Jesus his Son. If we claim to be sinless, we are self-deceived and strangers to the truth. If we confess our sins, he is just, and may be trusted to forgive our sins and cleanse us from every kind of wrong."

Jay was unaware of what they were doing for the next few minutes; the words from the Bible kept going through his mind. 'If—if—if.' 'If we walk in the light, if we confess our sins.' He wasn't sure Mr Barnard's message, God's message, was the way he wanted, for it didn't seem to promise him forgiveness, it didn't say he was clean from his sins. Before the promise of these things it had put 'walk in the light, confess'.

They all pushed into the kitchen. Jay joined in the refreshments but he had no heart for the plans they were discussing, he no longer wanted his voice to be heard.

"Well," said Mr Barnard, opening a packet of crisps, "let's get down to it. Hovant boys C.I.D. What about some constructive ideas."

"You know what, sir," said Peter; "they didn't want anyone knowing who they were. I mean, this person who put the telegrams in your doors—he didn't want you or Mr Lewis to see him."

Jay was fascinated despite his fears.

"How d'you make that out, Peter?" queried Mr Barnard.

"Well it's easy. You were all at church, so there

was no-one to see this person; and the other one was meant to come when everyone was in bed."

"Mm, I see what you mean. Yes, that's a good point. Why don't people want to be seen?"

"Doing wrong things, I guess," suggested Tony.

"What's wrong in delivering telegrams?" Jay was nettled, still struggling to justify his actions.

"Tell you another thing sir." John was looking serious. "It's someone who knows about you and the Lewises."

They were all alert at this suggestion.

"Someone who knows about us, eh? How about that, Jay? D'you agree?" Mr Barnard looked straight at Jay. "Someone who knows the Barnards go to church. Yes, I think John's got another good point there. We'll put those down." He opened his notebook, while the boys stood round eagerly. "What would you deduce from that?"

Vince looked at Jay. They both knew the answer.

"Must be someone in Hovant," said John slowly.

"Yeh, 'course," the others chimed in. And yet something about the very idea alarmed them. Anyone could be suspect.

"That narrows our field then," commented Mr Barnard. "Time to go home. Now what can we do before next week? I'll be contacting the post office. Do you know what your father's doing, Jay?"

Jay started. "Oh no, sir, no. I mean I don't know."

On the way home Vince was exuberant. "When we going to do others?" he demanded.

"We're not."

"Who said?"

"I'm going to put them back."

"What you want to do that for?" Vince was getting annoyed.

"Someone'll catch us, that's why."

"What, you scared?"

"No, I'm not. I just decided to put them back. I found them, so I'm the one can put them back." Jay walked ahead stubbornly, an unhappy expression on his face.

"That's not fair. That's rotten." They stood outside Jay's gate.

"See you," said Jay lamely. So there was even a barrier between him and Vince. He went indoors without looking back.

Mr Lewis was having a cup of tea before cycling the six miles to Ellis's.

"We had some supper with Mr Barnard." Jay declined the offer of a drink.

"You had a good time?" asked his father.

"It was O.K. We did codes. He showed us his telegram. Jay looked down at the table. Alone with his father he might have told the whole story, but with his grandmother there the confession was too difficult.

In his room he glanced at the secret drawer. Yes, he'd made up his mind to take the rest back; then he'd be finished with it. No, he knew that wasn't true; he wouldn't be finished with it. But he'd be doing the best thing. That wasn't true either. The best, the right thing was to bring the whole matter to the light.

Mr Barnard had asked them to read the first chapter of the first of John's letters in the New Testament before going to bed. Jay took up his Bible and found the place, not sure that he wanted to be reminded of the message.

CHAPTER TWELVE

WAYLAID

The wind was brisk, coming in short gusts which twisted the branches, whipped at the clothes-line next door, sent the evening clouds scudding across the sky. Jay descended the roof, chilly even in his thick jersey and jeans. He stood erect on the framework over the garden gates between eight and nine Fortune Row, feeling the wind buffeting him, exhilarated by its inability to daunt him. When he returned it would be dark and he would not be able to see the outline of the wood lintel on the edge of the slated roofs, but would have to trust to his sense of direction and touch. The thought of the lurking danger excited him.

Vince appeared at the window, his white teeth showing up against his dusky skin. Jay waited for him to descend the roof, then together they followed the familiar route, clambering silently over the shed, and disappearing through the gate onto the riverside path.

"Tell you something'." Vince was more than usually lively.

"Sh," cautioned Jay, "what?" The wind in the trees by the river, the movement of the water were all whispering voices, and you couldn't talk in a normal tone by the river at night.

"Somethin'," laughed Vince.

Jay wondered what exciting event at number ten could make Vince on top of the world. Or was Vince having his own back for Jay's decision to return the remainder of the telegrams? Was he taking plans into his own hands? Jay felt the packet of envelopes beneath his jersey, relieved that at last he could be shot of them.

They reached the tree, its branches strange and dim in the twilight.

"I'll put them back just like I found them." He was half talking to himself as he shook the envelopes free of the plastic bag into the cavity of the trunk. Vince directed the beam of his lamp into the dark interior.

"Wish I could find my torch," said Jay with a last look at the telegrams.

"Come on," urged Vince, full of his own surprise, and Jay, done with the telegrams, was prepared to make the most of the outing.

When they arrived at the backwater, Jay drew *The Henty* from her gloomy hiding-place. The sound of the water against her, the musty smell of rotting undergrowth excited him.

Vince was the first on board. "We'll take her to the bridge; it's best there for fishing."

Jay took the paddle and guided *The Henty* out of the closeness of the backwater to the main stream of the Ander. It was hard work getting the boat to the bridge with only one paddle and the breeze against them. The exertion warmed him and helped him to shake off the worries of the previous evening. They steered *The Henty* against the bridge out of sight of the fallen tree. Jay felt in the bottom of the boat for his fishing tackle.

"See." Vince stood up, rocking the boat with his sudden movement.

"Pack it up," complained Jay. Then he stared at the rod in Vince's grasp. Dark as it was, it was plain to him that this was not the familiar rod that Vince handled, but something superb and gleaming, a jewel of a rod, such as neither of them ever expected to possess. A small jealousy crept into Jay's heart as Vince displayed his treasure; he eyed the shining metal band, the polished wood.

"Where'd you get it?"

"It's a smasher. Whee-ee." Vince whipped it through the air.

"Where?" Jay was alarmed.

"From Stan."

"Stan?"

"Yeh. He's gone to his uncle's for the weekend. His uncle's got a Jag."

"But Stan wouldn't——"

"His mum and dad've gone as well." Vince caressed the rod proudly. "I borrowed it just for tonight. You have first go."

Jay held on to his own rod with its tangled twine that was slimy to the touch. Something was wrong, of that he was sure.

"Go on; you could cast it fine from the bridge."

Jay made no move, and he was feeling cold again. The sound of the wind in the trees made him afraid. "Did he lend it to you?" He knew the whole idea was ridiculous; Stan hardly favoured them with a look, and yet there was a chance that everything was above board.

"He keeps it in the shed; there's hooks in the wall

to hold it." Vince stretched his arm along the length of it. "His dad's got one as well."

"When did you get it?"

"S'afternoon. After tea. I went along with my mum; she's looking after their cat and the rabbits." Vince was not at ease, trying hard to justify his action.

"How did you get it to the boat? Why did you bring it here?"

"I put it outside their garden gate and then brought it along to *The Henty* afterwards, of course. Well, I can put it back, can't I? My mum's got the key." Vince's voice rose angrily as he sensed Jay's disapproval.

"Suppose someone sees it's not in the shed?"

"There's no-one," answered Vince scornfully. "Go on; you have a go."

"No." Jay drew back, making the boat lurch. The whole evening was threatened, and not just the evening, but him and Vince.

"Why not?"

Jay clenched his fists round his poor specimen of a fishing rod. "I'm not going to."

Vince flew into a rage. He had been sure Jay would admire his cleverness, would fall under the spell of the expensive rod, as he had done. And what right had Jay to think it was wrong?

Jay let his rod fall into the boat. "Let's take *The Henty* back."

Vince scrambled ashore. "You c'n do it by yourself. I'm fishing."

Jay had no wish to go on his own. There was something threatening about the backwater at night, but he wasn't going to let Vince think he minded. "Suit yourself; we'll leave her by the bridge. I'm going home."

"You rotten thing!" flared Vince.

Jay got out of the boat and proceeded to secure her by the bridge. "We can put Stan's rod back now."

"No we can't." Vince resented being told what to do.

"You've got to. You can get over the fence, and I'll hand you the rod."

There was no arguing with Jay when he gave orders like that. Vince retrieved his lamp from the boat and stood sulkily beside Jay. When he thought he had Jay with him, it had seemed worth risking taking the rod. And there wasn't really any danger. Jay set out for home, with Vince following close behind. As they neared the tree Jay slowed his pace.

"Give us a bit of light," he mumbled.

Vince turned the beam on the trunk. "I'll hold it," offered Jay, knowing Vince might find difficulty managing Stan's fishing rod, and wanting to make amends for his way of speaking to Vince. He took the lamp, showing the way for Vince, then directed the light for a last look at the telegrams.

"They've gone!" The beam searched the emptiness of the cavity, but there was no sign of the telegrams.

Vince came close, their quarrel over the fishing rod forgotten in the unwelcome knowledge that someone else had been along the river's edge, that that someone might still be around.

"What we going to do?" whispered Vince.

There was nothing they could do. "Let's go," said Jay. As he clambered down onto the path, he heard

Vince gasp, and the next moment he himself was seized from behind and a hand pressed over his eyes. The lamp was jerked out of his grasp.

"Got you," said his assailant.

"So you're the clever chaps who snoop around at night." It was the other one speaking, the one who Jay guessed must be holding onto Vince. Jay remembered the rod, Stan's spanking new fishing rod that Vince was holding. Suppose something happened to it?

"Been fishing?" Still it was the other speaking. "Nice rod. Your dad's?"

"No." Vince's voice was small.

Jay made a struggle to get free, but the arms about him were too strong.

"Whose, then?"

"Friend," said Vince.

"Mm, borrowed. Too bad if something happened to it. Who's your friend?"

"Nothing to do with you." Vince was angry and frightened.

"Won't speak, eh?"

"Oh, oh."

Jay heard Vince's sharp cry of pain. "Leave him alone," he cried, but the only answer to his plea was a tightening of the grip on his own body.

"I'm asking you."

"Oh—oh—oh. Stan Richards," said Vince pitifully.

"Well, well. Didn't know Stan had such nice friends."

Jay was more scared than ever. Vince couldn't possibly get out of things now; there'd be no getting the rod back without anyone knowing.

"Suppose I do you a favour and take it back for you."

"No, you can't." Vince's voice betrayed his fear. "He's gone away; he doesn't want it till Monday."

"Please God, make him let Vince go." It was the only prayer Jay could think of.

"Well, we'll make a deal," continued Vince's captor. "You keep your mouth shut about those envelopes you've just deposited in this old tree, and we'll keep quiet about your stealing this rod."

"I didn't steal it."

"A deal I said. And that goes for the two of you. Come on."

"Oh—oh."

Jay guessed he was twisting Vince's arm. He felt helpless.

"Come on," insisted Vince's tormentor. "Promise."

"O.K." There was despair in Vince's submission.

"And your pal."

Jay knew he couldn't hold out, he'd have to promise. The pressure of the hand across his eyes was making him feel dizzy. And yet he had to make some effort.

"I won't."

"Cheeky. Don't think we don't know who you are, Mister Jay Lewis."

Jay remembered his torch, with its name label. There was no way of escape. "O.K."

"And if you so much as breathe a word, your precious boat's going to be broken up.

"No." But Jay's voice was lost in the night. He'd promise, he'd have to, to keep *The Henty* safe.

"I'll give your kind regards to Stan. Now get going."

"I got to have my lamp," pleaded Vince.

For answer Jay heard a boot against the lamp at his feet. There was a strong kick, almost taking Jay with its force, and then a loud splash as the lamp went into the river. All Jay's earlier anger at Vince was gone. Vince was in a fix, he'd lost his lamp, he couldn't return the rod to the Richards, and two unknown people knew, knew about Vince and him.

"Get going, and don't look round."

The hand was removed from his eyes. There was a rustling and scuffling, then once more Jay and Vince were alone.

Vince could hardly restrain his tears. "I lost my lamp. My dad'll be mad." And there was nothing Jay could do to console him. "If they smash up *The Henty*, I'll——"

"Come on," encouraged Jay, though he felt anything but cheerful.

Through the garden, over the shed and onto the slates, no longer the jaunty pair pleased with their ability to outwit their elders. Jay watched Vince's shadowy form disappear through the bedroom window and then he was on his own. Alone he could not so easily banish the words Mr Barnard had read to them, 'Here is the message.' And now it was too late. They'd promised not to tell anyone about the telegrams; now it was too late to confess to his father.

He crept over the narrow bridge between the houses. This time there was no light shining from his grandmother's room. The dull misery at his heart tormented him. What was he to do? Just wait until someone found him out? He felt too ashamed to pray, and yet so often his father had told him God was more willing to listen than we are to speak to Him.

Now he was safe in his own room, but that did nothing to lighten the weight of his troubles. Standing by the window he wondered how he could begin to explain to God about it. But then God knew, He knew all about it. There was no need to go over it all, only to be sorry for the wrong things he'd done and be willing to do right things, to ask to be forgiven. For a long time he lay awake, battling with the temptation to withdraw his request to be shown the right thing to do, lest it should prove too difficult, then feeling curious as to how God would sort things out.

CHAPTER THIRTEEN

MENDER OF CHAIRS

There was no sign of Vince on Saturday morning, and Jay hung around the house unable to settle to anything, half expecting God to do something wonderful. The thought of what God might reveal made him apprehensive, but the morning wore on and nothing out of the ordinary occurred in Fortune Row. Jay decided that, if his father suggested an. outing, he'd give Vince a knock and invite him too. Vince's non-appearance worried him. On the other hand it might be better alone with his father.

At half past two Mr Lewis came downstairs for his meal. Jay, still restless, watched his grandmother take the hot plate from the oven and place it on the table.

"I'll just be going along to the shop. Jay, you can clear the table and leave the things for me to wash."

"O.K." He waited for her to go out of the kitchen. "Are we going out, Dad?"

"Did you want to?"

"Dunno, really."

"No Vince today?"

"No."

"I ought to finish those chairs."

"I thought you'd done that."

"I did one, but the others'll go the same way if I don't do something about it."

"Oh." Jay frowned.

"What about giving me a hand." Mr Lewis waited knowing Jay's reluctance to be tied down to anything he didn't fancy.

"O.K., Dad."

The shed was warm; everything about it was reassuring and familiar—bench, shelves, boxes, drawers with nails and screws, tool chest.

"Dad, suppose you've made a promise." Jay eyed his father warily, but Mr Lewis seemed to regard the conversation as perfectly normal, continuing to pass his hand over the smooth timber of the chair.

"Yes."

"And then you wish you hadn't."

"Mm. For any particular reason?"

"Well—well, because you think p'raps you ought to tell about something."

"That sort of promise; not a promise to do something."

"Oh no."

Mr Lewis looked up at Jay and smiled. "I thought for a moment you'd got yourself trapped. I was wondering what you'd promised to get done."

Jay laughed. "Not me."

"Suppose I make up a problem, and give you my verdict, then you see if it gives you your answer."

"Yeh." Jay felt lighthearted, no longer afraid to speak.

"And meanwhile you can be sanding down that chair. We'll give Gran a new set of furniture, time we've finished. Well now—school."

Jay smiled to himself. He was safe with school.

"Let me see. No, Jay. Now I think about it, I

believe a promise is a promise. I was going to say that promises made when you didn't really under-stand what they meant, or when you were forced into something, weren't quite the same as other promises. And in a way they aren't, but——"

Jay held the sandpaper, puzzled at his father's remark. "But suppose someone said they'd——"

"Yes, I know. It's difficult. And I don't like to think of anyone treating you badly, but it's part of learning to take the rough, having to be kicked around if we don't do what people say. And some-times fellows who are full of bravado when they've got a younger chap in their power aren't so very courageous when it comes to it. Stand up to them, ask God to help you, and stick to your guns."

Jay moved the sandpaper slowly over the scratched surface of the wooden chair. How could he and Vince have stood up to their attackers? Could they have refused to promise? The whole thing was that both of them had something to hide; they were afraid.

"Whatever you've promised, Jay, I think God regards it as a promise. If you've given your word, your word must stand."

So there was no easy way out. God wasn't going to provide a miraculous solution to his troubles.

"But that promise doesn't mean you can't tell God."

"No-o," said Jay slowly.

"Did the promise include me?"

Jay didn't look up. "Yes, Dad."

"I think I hear Gran coming." Mr Lewis righted the chair on which he had been working.

Mrs Lewis came into the garden. "Workers' tea

time." She looked at Jay as she placed a tray on the bench in the shed. "Just met Mrs Richards." Jay started. He watched his father take a large spoonful of sugar and empty it slowly into his cup of tea. Suddenly the shed seemed unbearably quiet, no moving of sandpaper against wood, no conversation, no shifting of tools in search of the right one. And all that filled Jay's mind was a fishing rod, a stolen rod. It seemed a long time before his grandmother spoke again.

"Mm. They got as far as the motorway. The back axle went."

"Oh dear," said Mr Lewis.

"They came back home by train. I reckon Stan will have to lend his father his motor-bike on Monday. Won't do that lad any harm to go on the bus. Bring the tray in when you've finished, Jay." She went back to the house.

Once again Jay found it difficult to talk; the relationship that had been easy a moment ago was gone. Stan had come between, Stan and his fishing rod. Suppose Stan was looking for the rod and it wasn't there? Vince, he'd be desperate about it. He'd know Stan was back; he'd have known this morning, because of his mother going to one Fortune Row to look after the animals.

"There is one other way, as I see it." Mr Lewis sipped his tea, conscious of the change in Jay. Jay selected a biscuit and pretended to be examining the layer of cream. "Stan's in it, it seems. I hope he doesn't bother you at school. He's not a bad fellow, really." Mr Lewis saw Jay flush. "But that wasn't what I was going to say. My suggestion is to go to whoever you promised and tell them that you now feel you've been wrong in promising and ask them to release you. Mind you, they still have the right to hold you to it. Could you say something like that to—Stan?"

"Oh it's not Stan, Dad," said Jay hurriedly.

Mr Lewis laughed. "That serves me right for asking questions. Well, that leaves you with telling God about it, and that's maybe enough. And I shall do the same."

"But you don't know anything." Jay managed a grin.

"I wouldn't say that."

Jay moved his finger in the fine sawdust that lay on the bench. It was such an ordinary thing to happen, a breakdown, but why did it have to happen this weekend? He thought of all that might result from it—a reported theft, Vince in trouble.

CHAPTER FOURTEEN

ROBINSON CRUSOE

Vince was waiting for him as usual on Sunday morning, an angry gleam in his eyes, indicating that he was not in a good mood.

"What happened?" asked Jay, fearing the worst.

"They came back. My mum told me."

"I know." Jay thrust his hands in his pockets, which brought to mind the fact that his Bible was indoors. "What you going to do?"

"Dunno." Vince kicked at a pebble. Everything he had reckoned would turn out interesting and exciting had gone wrong.

Jay regretted saying 'What are you going to do?' It sounded as though he intended to leave Vince in the lurch, and, despite the fact that he was still put out by Vince's action, he was prepared to stick by him. "What we going to do about them?" he asked.

Vince was still sore about the treatment he had received, about the loss of his lamp, about the way Jay had failed to appreciate his plan for their outing. He was frightened too; every moment held the possibility of discovery. "I'll get them," he said fiercely.

"We don't know who they are, so how can we?" Jay too was touchy, and his voice betrayed his impatience.

"I'll find out."

Jay knew Vince was bragging, bragging because he was worried and angry. The church was now in sight, but neither Jay nor Vince had given much thought to where they were going.

"We've got to find out about them," insisted Vince, meaning that he expected Jay to do something.

Jay thought hard. What clues had they got, what hope of tracing their assailants, when there were so many things they themselves didn't want discovered? Was there anything to give them a lead? He recalled the feel of that hand, a large hand, pressed hard over his eyes and forehead. But it was the other, the one who tackled Vince, who was the leader; he was the one who directed things. Was it just his torch that had betrayed them, or had they been seen replacing the telegrams? It all came down to the same point that John had made to Mr Barnard—'It's someone who knows about you and Mr Lewis'—only this time it was someone who knew about Jay Lewis and Vincent Collins. The thought was not very pleasant.

As they entered the church, Jay tried to dispel the gloomy forebodings, but they persisted, and the sight of Mr Barnard only served to make matters worse. Mr Lewis was playing a variation of the 'Trumpet Voluntary', a cheerful, exuberant tune in keeping with the bright sunlight that streamed through the narrow windows.

Later, as he and Vince settled in the small classroom at the rear of the church, he looked at Mr Barnard. It was odd to think that with a few words he could supply the answer to 'Who did it?'

"Got your Bible ready, Jay?"

"Oh no, sir. Sorry." Jay stole a glance at Vince.

Usually Vince recovered quickly from his bursts of anger, but this time he was really sunk in despair.

"What about you, Vince?" asked Mr Barnard.

"No," grunted Vince.

"We'll have Peter then; Robinson Crusoe's psalm."

"What, sir?" demanded Peter cheekily.

"No-one ever heard of Robinson Crusoe's psalm? No? Psalm fifty, and we'll have verse fifteen."

"O.K." Peter rustled the pages of his Bible. "Call upon me in the day of trouble: I will deliver thee," he read.

"Yes, that's where Robinson Crusoe opened his Bible."

Jay could not recall what happened when Robinson Crusoe read those words; in fact he couldn't remember ever coming across that bit in *Robinson Crusoe*. Now if Robinson Crusoe did what it said in the Bible, it should have solved his problem. But it didn't happen like that; he knew that much. No boat turned up the next day, or the next week, to rescue him. So did the Bible really mean it? Was it any good praying? He began to wonder how Mr Barnard would answer that question. Mr Barnard was holding a well-worn copy of *Robinson Crusoe* in his hand; the dust jacket with its gaudy illustration was torn. He began to read Robinson Crusoe's words.

" 'And I add this here, to hint to whoever shall read it whenever they come to a true sense of things, they will find deliverance from sin a much greater blessing than deliverance from affliction.' "

Jay stared at the book in Mr Barnard's hands. He disliked the old-fashioned words, but he knew what they meant.

On the way home he turned to Vince. "Say I ask my dad to write to Mr Henty and see if we can have *The Henty*. I bet he doesn't want it."

"Then it'ud be ours for keeps." Vince was all eagerness.

"Yeh."

"S'pose he says no."

"He won't," declared Jay, but he knew it was a risk. How else could he put the matter of *The Henty* right, and it had bothered him for some time that they had no right to the boat. If it hadn't been for Vince's taking the fishing rod, he might have let it slide. What was the difference between Vince 'borrowing' the rod and him 'borrowing' *The Henty*?

They parted at the gate and Jay went up to his room. The Bible which he had omitted to take with him was inside the cupboard. Turning the pages, he found Psalm fifty and verse fifteen. There it was as plain as could be: 'Call upon me in the day of trouble: I will deliver thee, and thou shalt glorify me.' He delved into the lower half of the cupboard in search of *Robinson Crusoe*, but even when he had retrieved his copy it took him some time to find the place Mr Barnard had mentioned. Mr Barnard had said it was for everyone, but his trouble was that he'd thought so much of his cleverness in finding the telegrams and outwitting people that it was hard for him to admit that his plans were heading for disaster. Nor did he want to admit, even to himself, that from the start he had known quite well that the right thing to do was to hand over the telegrams.

There in front of him was the challenge to take the same course as Robinson Crusoe, ask God about his trouble. It was nearly dinner time; Gran would be calling any time now. He'd wait till afterwards. No he wouldn't; he'd do it now. He'd ask God to help him with the tangle he'd got in over the telegrams, and he'd give up making excuses for what he had done. He'd always intended one day to own that he needed God to forgive him, and to accept that Jesus died on the cross instead of him. Now he realised that this was something so important it could not be put off.

"Please, Lord Jesus, forgive my not taking you as my Saviour before. But I will accept you now. I will. And will you somehow help me and Vince."

"Jay!"

"Coming, Gran! Robinson Crusoe!" he yelled, racing downstairs to the kitchen.

CHAPTER FIFTEEN

'THE HENTY'

"Dad." Jay poured a lavish helping of custard onto the apple tart, his mind occupied with Robinson Crusoe, telegrams, *The Henty*, fishing rods.

"Mm."

"D'you think if we wrote to Mr Henty he'd let us have his boat?"

His father and grandmother looked up, and Jay was aware of their scrutiny as he caught the drip of custard with his finger. "I mean me and Vince."

"Oh, just for a moment I wondered what Gran and I had to do with boating."

Jay laughed, anxious not to betray the importance of the matter. "He never took it when he moved from the farm."

"No point," said Mrs Lewis. "He doesn't live by the Ander any more. His boating days are over."

"That's true," added Mr Lewis.

"It's only an old boat actually." Jay waited, hoping his father would decide in favour of *The Henty*.

"Oh, I know it all right," remarked Mrs Lewis; "the one you and Vince have taken over."

"Well we thought if he didn't want it——"

"It's a poor, ramshackle bit of a boat," she added critically.

"It is not. It's O.K.," retorted Jay stoutly, forgetting that a moment previously he had admitted that *The Henty* was nothing much.

"And you want me to be your agent—that it?" enquired Mr Lewis.

"Yes, Dad." Jay held a spoonful of apple poised between the plate and his mouth, waiting and wanting to know what his father was going to do about *The Henty*.

"You and Vince plan to get in before anyone else."

"Yes, 'course."

"Well, nothing venture, nothing win."

"That's what we thought." Jay grinned, sure now that his father was on their side.

"Suppose we call on Mr Henty this afternoon, Vince as well. A two-mile walk over the fields'll be good exercise."

Jay reflected that it was certainly worth that to own *The Henty*. Imagine being sure she was your own, no need to hide her, no trying to question his conscience.

"O.K.," he agreed.

"I might have known it was something like that kept you out so long during the holidays," said Mrs Lewis.

"It was super." Jay laughed at her. "Bet you didn't really know.

"Well, maybe not," she admitted.

"Hallo, Mr Henty," greeted Mr Lewis; "I've brought two young men to see you."

Jay looked at Mr Henty and understood what his grandmother meant when she said his boating days were over. Mr Henty had difficulty rising from his chair, and, when he shook hands with Mr Lewis, Jay noticed that his hands were gnarled and stiff.

"Well that's good news now, that's good." Mr Henty let himself down slowly into the armchair. "Not often I get two young men to see me."

Jay felt bad about the reason for their visit.

"You're Jay, yes, I remember you."

"And he's Vince, Vincent Collins," said Jay.

"And you've had a longish walk, if I know your father."

"It was O.K.," said Vince.

"Not quite such a big place to look after now, Mr Lewis, but we like it." Mr Henty pointed to the garden that sloped down from the french windows. "Now what can I do for you? Ah, no, you can't kid me," he held up one bent hand and smiled knowingly, "that you have come all the way over here to see me for nothing."

Jay hesitated. His father had insisted that if he and Vince wanted the boat, then he and Vince must ask for it. "It was about your boat, Mr Henty," he began.

"Ah, yes."

"We, me and Vince, we wondered if you didn't want her any more if we could have her. Well, we have been using her in the holidays, but——"

"So you've had her out." Mr Henty raised his brows.

"You left her just by the bridge," said Jay.

"She's still good for a trip or two then."

"She's O.K." Vince watched Mr Henty.

"And we thought if you didn't want her——" Jay could think of nothing further to influence Mr Henty.

"We've called her *The Henty*," Vince butted in.

"You've called her *The Henty*." Mr Henty's voice was warm with enthusiasm. "Now that's something like it. What about that, Mr Lewis? Worth something to have a boat named after you. And a very good name, *The Henty*. Well, you've got me there, boys. I can't say no to *The Henty*."

"You mean we can have her?" asked Vince.

"That's about it."

"Aw, thanks, Mr Henty." Vince's eyes were dancing.

"*The Henty*, eh," he nodded his head in appreciation of the name.

"Thanks very much, Mr Henty," said Jay, thinking there ought to be something else you could say when you really were pleased.

"Tell you what we'll do." Mr Henty roused himself in his chair. "I'll make out a deed of gift, have things all shipshape. Jay, there's some paper over there on the table." He fumbled in his pocket for a pen while Jay fetched the paper.

"Now what shall we put? To Jay Lewis and Vincent Collins of Fortune Row, Hovant. Correct?"

"That's us," agreed Vince.

"Dated this nineteenth day of September, I William Henty hereby give the rowing-boat known as *The Henty*, clinker built in 1952. Signed William Henty. Does that suit you?"

"Yes thanks, Mr Henty; that makes her ours." Jay accepted the slip of paper eagerly.

"That makes her yours. Mind you, she could do with an overhaul; she's been lying idle for a year. Doesn't do a boat any good being idle, nor a body for that matter, eh, Mr Lewis?" The two men laughed together.

"We were thinking of painting her," boasted Jay.

"You'd paint the name on, of course." Again they saw that twinkle in his eye. "*The Henty*. Pretty good name, *The Henty*."

CHAPTER SIXTEEN

THE CLUE

There was the usual hubbub of conversation, the usual clatter of crockery, the usual warm smell of school dinners as Jay and Vince made their way into the dining hall.

Vince was about to make one of his comments on the menu, when he caught sight of Stan. He elbowed Jay to attract his attention. Stan had his brief-case tucked under his left arm, and with his dinner plate held in his right hand was heading for the table where members of the sixth form usually congregated. At the end of the service counter he stopped, put the plate down and sprinkled some vinegar on the greens, then, picking up the plate once more, continued on his way to the far table.

Something about the whole action suddenly struck Jay. He had it, the clue he was waiting for. He'd been staring at it, on Stan's right hand, as he raised the vinegar sprinkler. On the third finger a gold band with an oblong jet stone. Jay drew in his breath, making a soft whistling sound. It had been Stan's hand across his eyes, Stan's ring that had cut into the side of his nose. It was the sort of thing Stan would go in for. If only he could be alone now and work things out before he discussed it with Vince. The temptation to say to Vince 'Notice anything?' was almost too strong to be resisted. Another thought

came to him. He'd asked God for a clue to tell him
what was the right thing to do next, and here was a
super clue. Perhaps after all it wasn't just him being
clever in detecting it; perhaps it was God showing
it to him. On the other hand he couldn't help feeling
elated by this new evidence. If Vince came in after
tea, they'd do their homework together, unless they
were lucky enough not to have any. Vince was going
to be surprised.

"Come on," urged Vince, wondering why Jay was
hanging back.

Jay looked round. It was impossible to tell Vince
here; perhaps on the way home on the bus—but no,
he'd wait till tonight.

There was hardly space enough for the two of
them to do their homework in Jay's room, but they
preferred it to being downstairs. Here they could
be more certain of being on their own, here they were
aware of the river. Though *The Henty* and the fallen
tree were far beyond their vision, yet they were
conscious of their presence beyond the garden
fence.

Their homework dispensed with, Vince was all
for making a dash to *The Henty*.

"We got to do something else first," said Jay.

"Who said?" flashed Vince.

Jay laughed. "You know what John said at club
the other night, about it being someone who knows
about my dad and about Mr Barnard."

Amused at the recollection of how the two of them
had sat solemnly listening to the various suggestions,
Vince forgot to argue any more.

"Well, I reckon it's the same with those two who

got us on Friday. Tell you why. They knew about *The Henty*."

"Mm. They said they'd smash her if we told."

"And they knew Stan."

Vince glowered. "Yeh."

"Who'd you reckon?" asked Jay.

"I dunno."

"Go on; guess who one of them is," insisted Jay.

Vince searched his head. "They were rotten so-and-so's," he said viciously.

"Stan," announced Jay triumphantly.

Vince failed to be impressed. " 'Course it's not Stan, you fathead."

"Why not?"

"Well, what my one said about taking the rod back to him."

"That was just covering up; your one was laughing his head off because all the time Stan was with me."

Vince frowned. "Well you never said before."

"I know," admitted Jay. "I never thought of him, not till dinner time." He leant closer to Vince. "You remember him putting his plate down——"

Vince placed an imaginary plate on the table, sprinkled it liberally with imaginary vinegar, and then picked it up with all the mannerisms of Stan. It was so like Stan that Jay laughed noisily.

"He didn't see us," confided Jay.

"He's a bighead," declared Vince. "Anyway, why's it him?"

"I was watching him, and suddenly I saw this ring. It's on his right hand, one of those big, posh ones."

Vince held out his right hand, viewing a ring.

"And d'you know what?" whispered Jay. "The person who held me, he had a ring. When his hand was over my eyes, it pressed against my nose, and it jolly well hurt." Jay rubbed his nose. "It was just there."

Vince stared at him. He wasn't sure that he wanted it to be Stan. It didn't help; it made things worse.

"I'll tell you something else," continued Jay. "It was your one did all the talking; that was because they didn't want us to recognise Stan."

"Yeh. Mine was the worst," agreed Vince. "Cor, what we going to do?"

Jay was not sure that Vince was going to approve of his decision, but he had made up his mind, and nothing Vince had to say was going to move him. It was the only thing, the right thing. "We're going to Stan's," he said curtly.

"We're not." Vince was up in arms.

"Who says we're not?"

"It's crazy."

" 'Tisn't," retorted Jay. "We tell him we know it was him the other night, then we say you're sorry about taking the fishing rod."

Vince looked away.

"And we say we reckon he ought to get you a new lamp, and that someone ought to know about those telegrams. So we want him to let us off our promise."

"He ought to get me a lamp," scowled Vince.

"I thought of another thing." Jay was obviously pleased with his ideas. "When they made us promise to keep quiet about the telegrams, bet they didn't know we'd done two of them; but they think they've got them all."

"Yeh." Vince was gloating over the thought. "Bet they think they're O.K. When we going to Stan's?"

"Now, of course." Jay hesitated. There was something else he had to tell Vince. "If he lets us off the promise, I'm going to tell my dad it was me put them—you know, Mr Barnard's and ours. I shan't say it was you, not if you don't want."

"It was you and me did it," said Vince, "so you can say it was me."

CHAPTER SEVENTEEN

STAN

"I'm going with Vince," Jay called to his grand-mother as he closed the front door. At the end of Fortune Row he was half tempted to postpone the visit to Stan, and spend an hour in *The Henty*. It was that sort of an evening, a river evening. But he had settled with himself to face Stan at the first oppor-tunity, and that was now. If Stan was out, then they would have the rest of the evening in *The Henty*. All of him craved for the freedom of the Ander, the feel of *The Henty*.

"Come on," he ordered Vince, pushing the gate of number one. Being at the end of the row, the Richards' house had a strip of garden at the side where Mr Richards had built a garage which still looked new and out of keeping with the rest of Fortune Row.

Jay held the knocker in his hand. "Please God, will you help me—and Vince," he prayed, then it occurred to him that Stan would be in need of help too, but he did not add a prayer for him.

"Go on," urged Vince.

Jay rapped twice, and it seemed as though the sound would rouse all Fortune Row, since the street was exceptionally quiet.

Mrs Richards opened the door, drying her hands on a teacloth. "Oh, it's you. What d'you want, love?" She was plump and cheery, her hair a little untidy.

"We wanted to see Stan about something." Jay was hot; he could feel the perspiration on his forehead.

"He's in the garage. Here, you come through the house. That's no bother." They followed her into the kitchen.

"Stan," she called from the back door, "someone to see you. There you are, boys; you go out and find him, while I finish in here. He'll be tinkering with his bike."

Vince kept close to Jay as they went out to the garage. There was no going back now, and they had need of each other's support. The back doors of the garage were wide open onto the garden, letting in the evening sun. Stan, hands at his side, was looking critically at his motor-bike.

"Hallo," said Jay, thinking that Stan must have heard his mother calling and could at least have come out to them. He did look up at Jay's greeting, but, half shadowed as he was by the garage door, it was impossible to tell whether any flicker of alarm showed in his dark eyes.

Jay, held back by a sudden fear that what he had been sure was right might turn out to be rather silly, hesitated. "Er—we, we've got something to discuss with you."

Stan said nothing, nothing at all, only turned from his swift glance at his visitors to surveying the motor-bike once more.

Jay's anger was roused; his natural stubbornness made him dig in his heels. "There's one or two things," he added almost rudely.

"Yeh," supplied Vince.

"Such as?" Stan made a slight adjustment to the mirror, his careless attitude adding fuel to Jay's anger.

"Well, we happen to know it was you set on us."

"Set on you? Oh, come off it, you kids." From his five foot ten he looked down at Vince.

Jay lost his temper. "That's what we said." Suppose Vince was a bit of a shrimp, that didn't give Stan the right to smirk at him like that. But one glance at Vince and Jay's temper evaporated; he had no need to champion Vince. There were times when Vince was as bold and as cheeky as anyone. And just now his attitude was a perfect imitation of Stan's. It was a pity Stan couldn't appreciate how funny it was.

"That's what we said," repeated Jay.

"You don't expect anyone to swallow that yarn," said Stan scornfully, "and in any case I didn't happen to be around on Friday evening."

"I never said anything about Friday," intervened Jay quickly. Now he felt cool, alert, while Stan, confused by his mistake, raised his hand to his face. Jay saw the ring, and his determination was renewed. Friday, he thought, it was funny about Friday; Robinson Crusoe and Man Friday. He wasn't scared of Stan now; Stan had given himself away. "And you were there. You had a breakdown, and you were in Hovant."

"Half past ten, when small boys are in bed. You can check the time if you must." Stan had regained his composure.

Jay was riled at his quick recovery. "I happen to know it was your hand over my eyes—your ring."

"D'you think you can stand there and accuse me of beating you up?"

Jay was sure Stan went quite white; at least he was sure Stan ought to have blanched. Stan concentrated on the bike once more.

"There was something else," pursued Jay. "Vince has come to apologise for taking your rod."

Stan looked round, completely taken aback.

"Yeh, I'm sorry I pinched your rod. I was only going to borrow it just for——" His apology tailed off.

"Did you get it back all right?" asked Jay.

"I haven't a clue what you're blathering about."

"Oh," said Jay. How was it that Stan had got the upper hand again? He braced himself against defeat.

"What we really came about was to ask you and your friend if you would let us off the promise we made. You know, you made us promise not to tell about the telegrams. We don't think we ought to keep quiet about them."

"Sounds fine coming from you. One minute you admit swiping my fishing gear, the next you've got some precious sense of duty about some telegrams."

"I know," Jay refused to be daunted, "but will you let us off our promise. You made us promise, there was two of you, and you're——"

"Oh get shifted, for heaven's sake. I'm going out. You bore me stiff with your stupid tales."

"You won't let us off?" persisted Jay.

"We reckon those people ought to have their telegrams," added Vince.

"Telegrams? Whose telegrams?" Stan started up the motor-bike. "There's no telegrams, you——"

"You mean you've scrubbed them like you did my lamp." Vince was shouting against the noise of the bike.

Stan switched it off. "Drop it, you silly fools, can't you." His voice was quiet and intense, his dark hair falling over his forehead.

"We want to know tomorrow, at school. We know you'll have to ask the other person as well, so we'll give you till tomorrow. And it was you on Friday night."

"Let's go out the back gate." Vince was thinking of *The Henty*. Stan had made it quite plain that he had nothing more to say to them.

As they came out of the shadow of the garage door and onto the garden path, Jay saw Mrs Richards at the kitchen door. She was shaking a cloth, a blue-squared table cloth, but then she could also have been listening.

Now for *The Henty*; no longer any need to hide her. With Mr Henty's written deed of gift they could moor her close at hand, brag about their new possession, renovate her without any fear of losing her.

CHAPTER EIGHTEEN

'THE HENTY' IN DANGER

That Stan made no move to contact them at school on Tuesday surprised and disturbed Jay, for he figured they had Stan neatly trapped. On the only occasion when they caught sight of him during the day, he appeared unruffled. There seemed to be no way of getting at him. And yet Stan's attitude of unconcern intrigued Jay; perhaps it covered a more complicated mystery, something really big. If that was so, then no-one was going to stop him and Vince from pursuing it. Jay's mind filled with wild ideas; he imagined super roles for himself and Vince—detectives, champions, heroes. There was one problem. He had been sure God would reward him by making Stan release them from their promise, but Stan had not relented. So what did they do? What could they do? Then he realised they did have one more way of forcing Stan's hand, by telling him of the two telegrams they had delivered. That would make Stan see that the telegrams couldn't be kept secret. And if he tried to palm them off by saying it was all fairy tales, then it was possible for them to produce the actual evidence.

Meanwhile there were other exciting things to occupy them—there was *The Henty*. Despite their proud boast of making her shipshape, neither Jay nor Vince had any flair for such tasks, so Mr Lewis's offer to give *The Henty* an overhaul was more than welcome. The only thing was, they wanted it done at once, not at some vague date in the future.

Jay wasted no time in putting in his request when he got home from school. "Dad, could we do *The Henty* tonight?"

"Tonight?"

"Yes, Dad. We haven't got any homework——"

"Sure?"

" 'Course. And tomorrow we might get loads, and Thursday's club——"

"Looks as though it had better be tonight."

"Thanks, Dad. I'll go and tell Vince."

"Now half a minute, Jay."

Jay halted. Was there going to be some objection, a lecture, a condition.

"Don't expect the job finished in an evening. If I'm going to give you a hand, then we're going to do it properly. It's not just a case of getting out there with a tin of paint and covering up the dodgy parts of the boat."

"No, I know, Dad." Jay's voice betrayed his impatience. He just wanted to get out by the Ander, and start on something, whatever it was.

"There'll be some repairs no doubt. Carpentry takes time, and not any timber will do. I'll come out after tea and we'll see what needs doing. That sounds like Gran calling us."

Over tea, Jay could hardly contain his eagerness to start on *The Henty*, especially painting in her name with, perhaps, their own names underneath: Lewis and Collins.

"Go on now," said Mr Lewis; "fetch Vince, and I'll meet you out there."

"If we still had our garden gate you wouldn't have to go all round the end," remarked Jay slyly.

His grandmother gave him a stern look. "It's bad enough as it is, not knowing where you are; with this *Henty*, as you call the thing, and the gate always there, no-one would ever know what you were up to. Beside it might be a nine days' wonder."

" 'Course it won't," retorted Jay.

"We'll see. And don't you be letting your father do all the work." She pointed at Jay with the knife in her hand. "People that have boats should be prepared to look after them."

"We've had *The Henty* all the summer," laughed Jay. It was amusing letting her know now, though before it had been exciting keeping the matter to themselves.

"That's what it was." She collected the empty plates while Jay hurried out into Fortune Row to call for Vince. Vince probably wouldn't tell them much at home; they were always too busy to listen to his exploits. Jay realised that even his grandmother's criticisms meant in a queer way that she was interested in *The Henty*.

Jay waited a few minutes while Vince finished his tea, then the two went through the garden. They had moored *The Henty* by the tree that came halfway between their homes, as a sign that she was their joint possession. As they came onto the river path they caught sight of Mr Lewis rounding the corner by Stan's back garden, a bag of tools in his hand.

"Hi, Dad," yelled Jay.

They ran towards him.

"Hallo, Vince. Ready for the fray?" greeted Mr Lewis.

"Sure, Mr Lewis."

"Sooner we start, the better for you two—that it?"

They laughed and raced to the water's edge, each wanting to be first to reach *The Henty*. Jay was there first, then he turned to face Vince.

"She's not there. *The Henty*'s gone."

The three of them looked this way and that, scanning the whole stretch of the Ander, but not a single craft was in sight.

"She's gone." There was dismay in Vince's voice. Jay clenched his fist. Suddenly he was afraid, afraid because he could hear again the voice of Vince's assailant saying 'Your precious boat's going to be broken up', afraid because he now realised the sort of enemies he and Vince were up against. *The Henty* broken up just as she was theirs. "Oh, please God, don't let her be broken up; don't let *The Henty* be gone."

They stood mute by the water's edge, straining their eyes for some glimpse of the boat that had come to mean so much to them. Mr Lewis stood a little apart, witness to the shock of their discovery, to the fact that it was something more than a vanished boat that disturbed them.

"This is where you left her?" he asked.

"Yes, Dad, right by this tree."

"You're quite sure."

"Of course, Dad." Jay's voice was sharp.

"Let's take a walk along."

"She cant've gone; she's ours now." Vince was stunned by the disappearance.

"Wait a second. Here, take my tools, Jay." Mrs Lewis stooped down to examine the ground. "It's as well to have a look around before we go any further."

"What d'you mean?" Jay was so distraught he had no heart for any detective larks.

"I mean it's possible there might have been some other boys after *The Henty*. Was that why you wanted Mr Henty's note?"

"No," said Jay. Strangely enough that had not been the thought uppermost in his mind. To meet that problem he had been prepared to rely on his own precautions. It was rather the sense that he was using *The Henty* under false pretences.

"If someone has moved her, it's as well to see if they've left their mark."

"That's right, Mr Lewis." Vince crouched down by the Ander, searching for evidence of the thief. But in the shadow of the tree, it was difficult to distinguish any footprints.

Mr Lewis straightened himself, scratched his head, then held his chin thoughtfully. "You're quite sure none of the others at the club would want to take her for a trip? We don't want to make a big thing of it, if someone is doing the very same thing as you two when you first took *The Henty*." He was trying to get them to reveal the secret fears that bothered them.

"They never knew about it," said Vince quickly. "They go down past the weir, John and Peter and the others."

Jay said nothing, only shifted the bag of tools to the other hand. What ought he to do? It wasn't right to deceive his father, nor was it right to break a promise. He was caught in a trap, a trap of his own making. Who was going to free him?

"I wouldn't be too sure of that, Vince," reasoned Mr Lewis. "You seem to know what they get up to, so the chances are they've got a pretty good idea of your doings. When you brought the boat here, did you row her right up to this spot?"

"Mm, we paddled her all the way. Me and Jay decided before we fetched her where we were going to moor her. We'd got it all fixed."

Mr Lewis noticed it was Vince doing all the talking, which wasn't the usual course of events. "So you don't reckon you left any footmarks, apart from when you landed. That right, Jay?"

"Yes," mumbled Jay, but his mind was still battling with Stan.

"And going back to my question, you two," Mr Lewis looked from one to the other, "you seem sure it wasn't someone at the club, which means of course that it has to be someone else. This someone—would he be connected with that promise you mentioned on Saturday, Jay?"

"Yes, Dad." Jay breathed more freely. At least his father understood that part of the difficulty.

"Mm. So you mustn't tell me."

Jay remembered that on Saturday, when he had assured his father that Stan had nothing to do with it, he had honestly believed what he said; it was only since then that Stan had come into the picture.

"Now." Mr Lewis was going about things in his usual reasoned way. "I think our culprit took *The Henty* by the tow rope; he didn't fancy trusting himself to her. In the direction of the bridge. One or two largish footprints; after that he kept more to the grass." Mr Lewis moved slowly ahead, while Jay and Vince exchanged glances. But they couldn't face the misery they saw revealed in each other's eyes. Jay thought of Stan at school, Stan unperturbed, ignoring them and all the while knowing about *The*

Henty, knowing what they would discover in the evening. How could anyone do it? His anger against Stan grew, fed by the thought that they might lose *The Henty*, that someone like Stan could rob them of all that *The Henty* meant to them.

"I was wondering about Stan," began Mr Lewis, turning to the two boys. Their startled look did not escape him. "But *The Henty* isn't up to his standard. I don't think he would fancy himself in Mr Henty's old boat."

Neither Jay nor Vince made any comment, and the three progressed along the river bank until the fallen tree came in sight. There had been no sign whatever of *The Henty*.

"He couldn't—I mean, they couldn't tow *The Henty* past there, Dad."

The three stood and viewed the upturned roots and the invading river that now filled each cavity made by the wrenching out of the roots. Baffled, they approached the tree, the tree that had been the start of all their troubles.

Vince suddenly thrust out his arm, pointing a little way off shore, too taken aback to speak.

"They—they've sunk her," choked Jay.

The bow of *The Henty*, tilting slightly out of the river, one moment revealed, the next covered by the moving water, held him. How like them to do it. The rotten beasts. All right, it was a warning. It was meant to say 'Beware, you kids; don't think you can play about with us. Keep your mouths shut'. Well, he'd teach Stan, he wasn't going to let him get away with sinking *The Henty*.

Mr Lewis stared out at the evidence of a boat, a boat intentionally submerged in the waters of the

Ander. How it had been accomplished wasn't the point just now; the point was, who could feel so strongly against Jay and Vince to do such a thing? Jay and Vince were inclined to be cheeky, they had a tendency to interfere in other people's affairs while at the same time demanding their own privacy.

"What are we going to do?" asked Jay quietly, his face set as he gazed at the wooden ridge that was all that could be seen of *The Henty*.

"I don't know, Jay. We're in a spot. I'll ask you one question. Just now you said 'They've sunk her', and you meant it. You meant more than one?"

"Yes, Dad."

"Do you know who 'they' are? No, let me put it like this: do you know both or all of them?"

"No, Dad."

"One of them?"

"Yes."

"Mm."

"Dad, are you going to do something about getting her out?"

"I don't know."

"Can't we do something now?" pleaded Vince.

"I'm afraid not, not without some help. And I haven't much time tonight."

"We could swim out to her," suggested Vince.

"We can't just leave her there, Dad."

"You'll do nothing, Jay. I'm not sure whether she has been holed, or whether something's been loaded into her to sink her."

"Oh, Dad." Jay was stunned by the hopelessness of the situation. Where did Robinson Crusoe's verse come in now? 'Call upon me in the day of trouble: I will deliver thee.'

"Let's get back and work something out," coaxed Mr Lewis.

"Can we stay a bit? We won't do anything about *The Henty*, honest."

"Well, all right. But don't stay too long," he advised.

'Call upon me in the day of trouble', thought Jay. It was a day of trouble, no doubt about that. So what should he do? Just talk.

"Dear God. It's *The Henty*, and me and Vince want her."

CHAPTER NINETEEN

TELEGRAMS AGAIN

They watched Mr Lewis go, then stood gazing at the ridge of wood that appeared above the water. The ripples of the Ander reflected the evening sun, but the peaceful scene held no charms for Jay and Vince. For them all the fun had gone out of life.

"Let's go and find Stan," decided Jay; "he's not going to get away with it."

"Yeh, let's," agreed Vince. "What we going to say to him?"

"Tell him we delivered those two, so it's no good him thinking he can hush everything up."

"That'll do him." Vince's eyes glistened angrily.

"Wish we knew what he's up to," Jay frowned. There were things Stan had already made out he didn't believe; suppose tonight was a repetition of his previous attitude.

The same thoughts were plaguing Vince. "S'pose he says it's all make up."

"We can prove it. There's my dad's telegram."

" 'Course." Vince was elated. "That'ud be it."

But Jay knew he could not ask his father for that telegram.

Vince was about to try the back gate to the Richards' garden but Jay would have none of it, so they proceeded to Fortune Row. As they came out onto the road they perceived Mrs Richards a few yards ahead.

"But she's going to see my mum," whispered Vince, dodging back out of sight; and sure enough she disappeared into number ten.

It was little more than half past six, yet so much had happened since teatime that it seemed later.

"Come on." Jay tried to dispel his nervousness as he opened the gate of number one. He certainly wasn't going to let Stan think he was scared. He rang the bell loud and long, then thrust his hands into his pockets and waited.

It was Stan who opened the door, but it was impossible to tell whether their re-appearance perturbed him.

"Oh, it's you," he said.

Jay stepped inside before Stan could object. "It's two things," he began, shouting a little to conceal his lack of confidence. "You've sunk our boat——"

"I wouldn't touch it with a barge pole," interrupted Stan scornfully, "and since when has the thing been yours?"

"Mr Henty gave it to us. We've got it in writing, so nobody's any right to touch our boat."

For a moment Stan looked the slightest bit abashed, then he shrugged his shoulders. "Nothing to do with me. Nothing you can do about it."

Jay glared at Stan. "My dad will . . ."

Stan half smiled as though this were the tack he expected from a kid who couldn't stand on his own feet. Jay reddened, annoyed with himself for resorting to such a measure. But what else could he and Vince do against Stan? Well they would do something;

they'd follow every clue, they'd get all the evidence, so that there was no way out for Stanley Richards.

"And the second thing"—Jay wished Stan wasn't so tall—"there was something we forgot to mention; we didn't put all the telegrams back."

He wished Stan had blanched, started, which by rights he ought to have done. But Stan never flinched, merely stood there with the faintest smile on his lips, still holding his fountain pen in his right hand. "We thought you would have heard by now about the other two."

"You really are clean crazy." Stan leant back against the wall, but his eyes were angry. "I don't know why I listen to you. Of all the feeble yarns, this takes the biscuit. Telegrams—I ask you! Where do I come in? First you accuse me of beating you up, then you come up with this fairy tale. You're up the loop. Two you didn't put back. Didn't put back where?"

"In the tree," said Jay, and Stan managed to look surprised and innocent. "We couldn't put them back —because we delivered them."

And he knew Stan was shaken this time; he knew those two telegrams mattered to Stan. "One was to Mr Barnard. He doesn't know it was us put it in his door. He told us about it at club, so we thought you might have heard."

"Marvellous what you cook up." Stan had re-gained his composure. "And the other one of these magic telegrams—who came in for that?"

Jay and Vince exchanged glances.

"It was for my father," said Jay.

Stan looked up suddenly from the fountain pen which he had been considering. "For Mr Lewis?

And what does he know about this fantastic telegram business?"

"Nothing, but he's going to. That's why we want you to let us off the promise. I want to tell him I put it there, before he goes to the post office. If I don't——"

Stan moistened his lips. "Want to confess like a good boy?" he said sarcastically.

Jay grew angrier. "Mr Barnard's going to the post office about his."

"And we want our boat," Vince chimed in; "we never said we wouldn't say anything about that. Mr Lewis knows what's happened to it."

"And this fishing rod of mine you sneaked off with?" There was the hint of a threat in Stan's voice.

"All right, you tell them about it if you like. I don't care," said Vince defiantly. "It's nothing to what you've done."

"Shut up, you little prig."

"We want to know tomorrow." Jay tried to make his voice sound firm. "When you've seen your friend."

"Oh, spare me any more. Who says there were any telegrams?"

"We got proof." Vince stuck his thumbs up. "We got his dad's telegram, and we got something else. We'll be seeing you."

CHAPTER TWENTY

SALVAGE OPERATION

Though Stan closed the door on them sharply, it was not until they reached Jay's house that they spoke to each other.

"Tell him that tomorrow," whispered Jay.

"About us copying them, yeh. He thinks we're done."

It still brought a sense of shame to Jay when he remembered unsealing the limp envelopes, and rather badly re-sealing them. Too late he realised that it would be obvious they had been tampered with. Even now Mr Barnard might be following up that line.

"If he doesn't let us off our promise, then we tell him we deliver the rest of the messages—or——" Messages—why did the word bring him up with a start? "Let's go and get a drink."

"I'm starving," said Vince. "We still got one card to play." He grinned at Jay.

Expecting them to come in with gloomy faces, Mrs Lewis had prepared some refreshment to solace them after the disaster to *The Henty*. "Your father told me," she said quietly. "Don't you worry, he'll get your boat back."

"D'you think he will?" asked Jay.

"Think! I know," she declared.

Re-assured, they sat at the kitchen table and enjoyed the squares of sticky gingerbread; with her hovering around they could make no mention of Stan, but their eyes spoke. Tomorrow, one card to play.

But once again Stan evaded them. They made every effort to contact him, without success.

Angry at the failure of their plans, Jay and Vince returned home and entered the kitchen of number seven to find Mr Lewis washing his hands at the sink, and Mrs Lewis ironing.

"Ah, there you are." Mr Lewis turned and regarded them with his sharp blue eyes, noting their despondent look. "We've got one bit of good news."

"What, Dad?"

"Well, as it was early closing for Mr Stanton, I got him and old Mr Haines to give me a hand with *The Henty*."

"Dad!"

"That's what the cleaning up is about." Mrs Lewis nodded her head in the direction of the sink.

"You got her?" asked Vince eagerly.

"We did."

"Dad, can we go and see her, now? Oh please, Dad."

"Tea first," said Mrs Lewis firmly, putting away the ironing things. "Once you get out there, you'll be gone for hours.

Jay made a face.

"She'll need a good drying out before we attempt any repairs." Mr Lewis tried to convey to them that it was useless to attempt to do anything to *The Henty* that evening.

"Is she holed?" enquired Vince.

"How did you get her out?" demanded Jay.

"She's not holed, and we freed her by sheer hard work. I believe whoever sunk her loaded her with stones and earth from the bank, plus a good helping of river water to add to the weight, then pushed her out until she was submerged."

"The rotten things," muttered Vince.

"You know, I've been thinking about *The Henty*." Mr Lewis held up his hands to ensure that he had removed all traces of dirt. "It came to me while we were salvaging her. But it's up to you."

"What, Dad?" Jay knew it was going to be something difficult, the way his father was hesitating, choosing his words, concentrating on drying his hands.

"Well—what about *The Henty* belonging to the club?"

Neither Jay nor Vince said a word. The idea appalled them. Give up *The Henty* just as she had been retrieved? They heard the clink of china as Mrs Lewis placed cups and saucers on the table.

"There's several reasons," continued Mr Lewis. "One practical one is that it will share the expense of renovating, and enable us to do a much better job on her. Things cost money. But there's another reason; I've been discussing it with Gran."

Jay knew it; he knew directly he walked in that they had been talking about something to do with him, and he was annoyed.

"It's this." Mr Lewis looked directly at Jay. "You could keep *The Henty* to yourselves and have quite a bit of fun. On the other hand if you shared the boat, if *The Henty* belonged to the club, you could still enjoy her, and into the bargain *The Henty* would be a great attraction, help Mr Barnard to get other boys along. *The Henty* would act as an invitation. Do you agree? Jay? Vince?"

Inside them both the struggle went on. The idea was not entirely new to Jay; it had crossed his own mind, but he had pushed it to one side.

"Guess so, Dad," he said reluctantly.

"It's up to you both, Vince as well."

Jay coloured at the hint of reproof, knowing that he often regarded the boat as more his than Vince's. "Vincy won't mind."

But Vince did mind. The secret outings, the partnership with Jay, the sense of ownership that had lasted so briefly—these were hard to relinquish.

"You see," explained Mr Lewis, "I'm very conscious that it could easily have been someone else who appropriated the boat and went along to Mr Henty."

"S'pose so," admitted Jay.

"Still, it's only an idea. You'd have the fun of presenting her."

"Caw!" exclaimed Vince, suddenly captivated by the idea.

"We might even have a plaque—presented by, Henty, Collins, and Lewis. You know I believe old Mr Henty would give you a sub if he thought *The Henty* was going to be used by the club; he might even rise to some decent oars."

"Would he?" asked Jay, seeing again the old man with gnarled hands and twinkling eyes.

"Nothing to stop us taking another walk over there at the weekend and discussing it with him."

"Then we could tell him what happened about, you know, being sunk," suggested Vince.

"Yes. That would interest him. He'll be pleased she's been salvaged."

"And we could tell Mr Barnard about it tomorrow." Vince was won over to the idea, unaware that there would be other battles within him for her ownership.

"I'd like to tidy her up a bit, but perhaps it's as well to let him know straightaway, if you've made up your mind."

Mrs Lewis kept glancing up at Jay as she laid the table, seeing the tug-of-war that was going on inside him.

"Just two things," cautioned Mr Lewis.

They waited, disliking conditions.

"If you give something, you give it. *The Henty* won't be yours; it'll be 'ours'."

"Suits me," said Vince with an effort, thrusting his hands into his pockets. "Where you got her now, Mr Lewis?"

"Up against your garden fence to give her a chance to dry out. I asked your mother's permission, and I put a notice on *The Henty*: 'Property of V. Collins and J. Lewis. Please do not touch'."

"Vince, you'd better go and ask if you can stop to tea," suggested Mrs Lewis.

"What was the other thing?" Jay looked down at his shoes.

"If you're going to mention it to Mr Barnard, then you're not to say anything to the others, you're not to disrupt the evening or spoil Mr Barnard's plans by getting the boys worked up about *The Henty*. It's Mr Barnard's job to tell them. I want a promise about that."

"O.K., we promise," said Jay for both of them, knowing that they would have done the very thing his father aimed at preventing.

"D'you understand why?"

"Sort of," admitted Jay.

"You might interrupt the message he wanted to get across, by side-tracking the boys into something else. It's a favourite pastime." He smiled at Jay.

"Bet they'll think it's a smashing idea," said Vince. Now that he could look forward to being the important donor of *The Henty* to the club, he could anticipate retailing her misadventures.

Jay still clung to *The Henty*. After tea they would be free to view their rescued boat, free to indulge in plans for presenting her to the club, free to air their real feelings. Stan was momentarily forgotten.

CHAPTER TWENTY-ONE

INTERROGATION

Jay was downstairs early on Thursday morning. His father was already seated at the table, scanning the headlines of the paper, while his grandmother was at the cooker supervising the breakfast preparations.

"Mm." She eyed him critically. "Still thinking of your boat?"

Jay laughed. He felt lighthearted, the threat of Stan and of discovery banished by the future of *The Henty*.

"Full of plans," she said.

"Yep. We know what we want to do, don't we, Dad?"

"Now you're down we might as well make a start on breakfast." She moved the porridge saucepan from the gas.

"Dad, do you really think Mr Henty would——"

"Can but try. He certainly fancied your naming the boat after him. Master stroke of persuasion telling him that."

Jay raised his head in the air in a gesture of pride. "Brains," he said.

"Humph," said Mrs Lewis. "More like cunning. He used to be interested in the boys of Hovant; had them over to the farm sometimes. Your father went several times."

"Vince and I reckoned we could spend some of the club time doing her up."

"That, Jay, is entirely up to Mr Barnard. You aren't leader yet," warned Mr Lewis.

"What else have you and Vince planned?" Mrs Lewis came across to the table and placed a bowl of porridge in front of each of them. For a few moments the three were occupied with sifting sugar and adding milk, but Jay's mind was full of *The Henty*. From the cooker came the soft sound of bacon sizzling in the frying-pan.

"I've been thinking."

Jay turned towards his grandmother, hoping she had no ideas for *The Henty*. He didn't want her to imagine she had any say in directing their plans for the boat. He saw her determined look, the short, dark hair about her thin, lined face, her piercing blue eyes on him while she held a spoonful of porridge halfway to her mouth.

"When was this?" Mr Lewis winked at Jay, who returned the signal. Whenever Mrs Lewis tended to get too serious, they laughed at her.

"When? Why, when you were out last night with your *Henty*." She ate the spoonful of porridge, ignoring their amusement.

She's got an idea about *The Henty*, thought Jay. Well *The Henty* was theirs. "What were you thinking about?" he asked her, grinning at his father.

"About that telegram."

The laughter went out of Jay's eyes, the colour crept up his neck, suffusing his face as he bent over the plate. He let the steam from the porridge come up to his face; nothing could make him redder than he was.

"Oh, the telegram," interjected Mr Lewis.

"That's what I said. I've been working it out, and I've narrowed it down—about the time it came, that is." She was enjoying the porridge, every spoonful of it, but for Jay no such pleasure remained.

"Mm, might prove useful." Mr Lewis was interested.

"You left earlier than usual to call on Charlie Foster. Remember?" She pointed her finger to accentuate the importance of her statement.

"Correct," Mr Lewis agreed. "And Jay went up to his room at a quarter to nine. Not that he went to bed then, but that's as may be."

Jay wanted to go on making a joke of it, gang up with his father in teasing his grandmother, but there was no longer any humour in the situation.

"Well about twenty to ten Mrs Barnard came round. I'd met her Monday, that was when she told me about the telegram, and I promised if she should want me to mind Robert while she took Susan to the dentist, I'd be willing, provided she let me know in good time. We had a cup of tea and she left at twenty-five past ten."

"What you're getting at is that the telegram was delivered between twenty-five past ten and twelve," said Mr Lewis.

"That it was. It was not on the mat when I said goodnight to Mrs Barnard," she affirmed. Jay relaxed. It was nothing; only what had been said before.

"Did you hear Mrs Barnard, Jay?" she enquired abruptly.

His fair skin showed the redness all too plainly, and his heart began pounding uncomfortably. Look up, he dare not, and he had made up his mind not to tell any lies.

"No," he said quietly.

"You didn't? Humph. She wasn't exactly quiet." They all knew Mrs Barnard's noisy voice and hearty laughter. "Then all I can say is you must have been sound asleep if that didn't rouse you."

Jay tried to smile, hoping that was the end of the matter, but his grandmother hadn't finished.

"I thought you were reading that night." He might have known she never forgot anything.

"Yes."

"And by the looks of you the next morning, you weren't asleep at half past nine, nor at half past ten, and if you didn't hear Mrs Barnard you certainly weren't awake." She took her plate and crossed to the gas cooker. Jay raised his eyes only to meet his father's searching gaze.

"In that case what were you doing?" she demanded.

"I was—out." Jay placed his spoon carefully on the plate, waiting for the row he knew he must expect.

"With Vince, I'll be bound." There was a sharpness in her voice.

"How did you manage that, Jay?" Mr Lewis asked.

"Down the roof and over to his place."

"And not the first time," added Mrs Lewis.

"What for?" Jay detected a note of anger in his father's tone.

"You went to your *Henty*. I might have known." Mrs Lewis came across with the plates of bacon.

"Is that right, Jay?"

"Yes, Dad." Perhaps now they would forget the telegram. He couldn't answer the two of them, his grandmother rattling out the questions, his father watching.

"Did you do this every night?"

"No, Dad. Not every night."

But when once his grandmother got a notion, she pursued it. It was a vain hope to expect she might be side-tracked by his nocturnal visits to *The Henty*.

"And when did you get back?"

"Well——"

"You'll answer me," she insisted.

"Your bedroom light was on." But suppose she thought he was out till midnight, there'd be more trouble. "It was when you went up with your hot-water bottle," he added hastily.

"And I never heard you?"

"I waited till you put it out, then I got in through the window."

"I reckon you did, too. Did you go straight to sleep?"

"No, not at once."

"Did you hear the letter-box?"

"No."

"Funny, neither did I. Though it's a fair job for anyone to let that flap down without it giving a good sharp click. And the telegram was on the mat, not stuck in the letter-box, so there had to be some sound. Did you hear me come up to bed?"

It would be so easy to get out of it with a lie, but he had heard her, the muffled sound of her slippered feet. "Yes," he whispered.

"Your ears were sharp enough for that. How come you missed——"

"Jay," interrupted Mr Lewis, "have you any idea who put that telegram on the mat?"

"Yes, Dad."

"And who delivered Mr Barnard's?"

"Yes."

"The same person?"

"Sort of."

"You don't have to tell me you put it on the mat and kept awake just to hear me find it." His grandmother's look was severe.

Jay toyed with the bacon.

"Is Gran right. Was it you, Jay?"

Jay saw the grieved expression in his father's face. "It was only for fun," he said lamely.

"Fun!" Now he knew his father was really angry. "That's not the point. The point is, how you got hold of them, who passed them on to you; that's the serious part. Here am I demanding an explanation from the Lisham Post Office, and all the time my own son can supply the information I want. Apart from putting me in a very difficult position, it's not my idea of a joke, nor did I expect that you would play that sort of a trick on your own family. Or on Mr Barnard. It's despicable."

Jay gulped. Couldn't they understand, it wasn't like that when he and Vince began it.

"It—it seemed O.K. when we did it."

"You and Vince," said his grandmother.

"Well, where did you get hold of them?" demanded Mr Lewis.

Jay looked at his father. "That was what I promised not to tell."

"I see."

"Something I see is that if he doesn't hurry he'll

miss the bus. Eat your breakfast," insisted Mrs Lewis.

"And I said a promise was a promise," said Mr Lewis quietly. "Odd there was just two weeks between the dates; more odd that there were just those two telegrams. Were there any others?"

"Yes."

"You haven't got those?"

"N-no."

"We'll leave it at that just now. But don't think we're going to leave it altogether."

Jay pushed back his chair. The joy had gone out of *The Henty*, out of everything.

"Jay, I'm trusting you that whatever is the right thing to do you'll do it, however difficult it is." Mr Lewis challenged Jay.

"Yes, Dad."

"Perhaps it'll teach you not to make such wicked promises," added his grandmother severely.

"I couldn't help it," he flared at her. He had had enough, he was in enough trouble without her rubbing it in.

"How was this?" asked Mr Lewis.

Jay stood there, trembling with temper. "Last Friday," he admitted reluctantly.

"At school?"

"No, I told you it wasn't." He still wasn't in control of his voice.

"While you were out with Vince at night," suggested Mrs Lewis.

"Yes."

"I don't like it, Jay." Mr Lewis shook his head. "I don't like it, because people who force you to promise things in order to hide their own wrong doing don't very often leave it at that. I don't like it, because it means you're connected with those who aren't very honest. You haven't been honest yourself. I'm going to ask God to show you what is the right thing to do, and to give you the courage to do it." He gave Jay a smile of encouragement. "When you think of it, we give Him some pretty sticky problems to sort out."

"Now get your things and go," ordered his grand-mother. "You'll have a fair yarn to tell Vince. Not that you've anything to boast of this time. Here's your sandwiches," she added more kindly.

Ashamed, he went into the hall, picked up his satchel and disappeared into Fortune Row.

CHAPTER TWENTY-TWO

THE CREW

Despite the unnerving questions of the morning, Jay was in high spirits at the prospect of club that evening, of impressing both Mr Barnard and the boys with their magnificent gift of *The Henty*. At the same time he did not forget his father's warning not to disrupt the evening, knowing that he would be expected to give a report of what happened.

Jay and Vince arrived early at the hall.

"Ah, hallo, Jay; hallo, Vince. What about giving me a hand?" suggested Mr Barnard.

"Sir," began Jay, unconcerned by the preparations for the evening's activities.

"Mm?" Mr Barnard moved a table against the wall to make more room.

"We've got something to tell you."

Mr Barnard looked across at them. It was a battle to hold their interest. They came, but that was all. Often as not their minds were occupied with other things, and always they withheld some part of themselves. For a moment his heart misgave him. Had they come early to say they were leaving the club? In such a small place as Hovant it was difficult to run anything for young people, and every member was vital; the loss of one would discourage the others.

"Yes, well let's have it."

"We've got something we want to present to the club," said Jay, taking the lead.

"Oh, sounds pretty interesting. Long time since anyone had a presentation for us." Mr Barnard rubbed his head and looked at the two boys.

"It's this boat, see," continued Jay.

"*The Henty*," added Vince proudly; "she's ours."

"A boat?" Mr Barnard stared at them, unbelieving. They grew more excited, pleased by the expression of amazement on his face.

"That's what we said." Jay laughed.

"Mr Henty gave it to me and Jay."

"And we thought—well it was my dad's idea really—he thought if we shared it with the club it might be—it might recruit others." Jay felt bad saying it, when never once before had he ever bothered about getting new members. He couldn't meet Mr Barnard's look.

"I should just say it would; a tremendous help. You've got me stumped. I don't know what to say. It's very kind of you."

"Dad said he'd give us a hand getting her done up."

"Well." Mr Barnard had still not recovered from his surprise. "I didn't expect this."

"*The Henty*'s outside my garden fence; we could go and have a look at her tonight." Vince saw no reason to postpone the inspection.

"Pre-view, eh?"

"Dad said that was up to you."

"Anything else he said?"

"Yeh," Jay grinned. "We weren't to tell the others."

Mr Barnard laughed. "That was very thoughtful of him."

"Dad thinks Mr Henty might give us some new oars when he knows the boat belongs to the club."

John and Peter entered the hall.

Mr Barnard signed to Jay and Vince not to say a word. "Maybe we will have an inspection," he whispered.

"Hallo," Jay greeted the two new arrivals, wondering what they would say when they heard the news.

By the time they met for biscuits and squash in the church kitchen, Jay realised the evening had meant more to him than usual. In surrendering his right to *The Henty*, he had gained a sense of belonging to the club.

"You done anything about the telegram, sir?" asked Tony.

"I have. Written to the post office, and received a reply. They want to inspect the telegram, check the details I gave them. Any of you had any bright ideas?"

Jay looked away.

"What about your father, Jay? I meant to have called to find out what progress he had made."

"He hasn't heard anything," said Jay abruptly. What would Mr Barnard think of him when he found out what he and Vince had done? Would his father tell Mr Barnard of the morning's conversation?

"Well, we haven't got much time for clue-hunting tonight,' declared Mr Barnard.

"Oh, sir," objected Alec.

"Something more important."

"What?" they cried.

"We are about to have a boat for——"

"A boat!"

There was an immediate uproar.

CHAPTER TWENTY-THREE

JAY

Jay closed his bedroom door and crossed to the window. The inspection of *The Henty* had been a real success; all of them had agreed that it was a great idea having a club boat and very decent of Jay and Vince to part with *The Henty*. Their enthusiasm had in some measure eased Jay's regrets. Mr Barnard's words came back to him, the things he had said about *The Henty*. He had talked about Peter being pleased for Jesus to use his boat, and that they also could let the Lord Jesus use their new boat. It seemed an odd idea when Mr Barnard first mentioned it, but now Jay began to grasp its meaning. In his heart he knew that giving *The Henty* to the club was the only way he would have let Jesus use the boat. Up till then he and Vince had wanted *The Henty* for themselves, and for no-one else. Mr Barnard said he considered *The Henty* as God's boat from now on, and that was something that had never occurred to Jay. *The Henty* had been very much Jay Lewis's boat. It came to him that he loved God very little. *The Henty* was for whoever joined the club; anyone who belonged had part in *The Henty*.

He looked out at the trees and his mind was back with the other problem. Only two weeks since he had been standing staring out at the drenching rain; two weeks since that blinding flash struck the tree. And

here in the room were copies of the remaining telegrams, undelivered messages. That message Mr
Barnard had read. This is the message, that God is
light. Was the lightning God's light? Had he meant
it to strike the tree? Jay turned away from the
window and sat on the edge of the bed. His father
would tell him to pray. How could he start?

"Please God . . ."

He looked miserably at the floor. "Please God, I
don't know what to do, and I'm scared about them
finding out, and about Mr Barnard knowing." He
thought for a moment. He did believe, he did trust
Jesus to forgive his sins, so that must include what
he'd done about the telegrams. "And please God,
will you stop me wanting *The Henty* back. Make her
your boat."

CHAPTER TWENTY-FOUR

STAN AGAIN

On Friday, the last lesson over, Jay and Vince made straight for the school cycle shed. Stan's motor-bike stood out among the assortment of pedal cycles, but they did not go over to it, only waited and watched while other boys collected their bikes. Jay was on edge, sure in his own mind that he must tackle Stan once more, yet unsure of the outcome of that meeting. So obsessed was he with the urgency of the matter that he could only pray, "Please God, will you make it so we can speak to Stan, and please make him listen and say yes."

When Stan arrived he was accompanied by three friends, and did not observe Jay and Vince. He strapped his brief-case to the carrier of his motor-bike while the other three unpadlocked their cycles. Jay knew he had to act. "Come on," he whispered to Vince.

"Not with them," objected Vince.

"It's no good waiting," protested Jay, and advanced towards Stan. "We've got to speak to you."

Stan made a gesture of impatience. "Oh, not you two again."

"He doesn't take your sort of passengers," laughed one of the other boys.

Jay pushed his hands into his pockets and tried to pull himself up to Stan's level. "You've got to let us off that promise," he demanded in a low voice.

"You make me mad."

Jay had bottled up his resentment against Stan for too long. "My dad knows it was me put the telegram in our house, and him and Mr Barnard have written to the post office——"

"So what!"

"And there's something else you don't know." All Jay's anger showed in his voice and attitude. "Me and Vince copied the others, and we're going to deliver them."

"Oh no you're not." It was out before Stan thought what he was saying.

"Oh yes we are," Vince chimed in, slipping imaginary telegrams into unseen letter-boxes. "Boing, boing."

In that moment Stan recovered himself. "Copied telegrams," he said disdainfully.

"Yeh, we got the lot," declared Vince.

"And the dates? They were all in August and September last year," added Jay.

"And who do you think is going to take any notice of a scruffy document written out by two crummy school kids?"

"They will; there's things 'ud make them," said Jay desperately, seeing that once more Stan was wriggling out of things.

"Can't you get it into your stupid heads that I wasn't even in Hovant last summer."

Foiled again. It was true. Stan's family only moved into Fortune Row at Easter. But they couldn't have lived far away, because Stan had been at school at Lisham when he and Vince first went there a year ago.

"You've got to let us off our promise," Jay insisted stubbornly.

"Get out of my way, you little pests."

"No." Jay stood his ground.

"You cheeky little devil. Scram." Stan went to push Jay out of his path.

"What's the game?" It was one of the masters. Jay was flushed, breathing hard.

"The little so-and-so's were tampering with my bike."

"I never touched it," denied Jay hotly.

"The others, they were here just now; they'll tell you. They were cadging a lift," declared Stan.

"Is that right?" The master turned to Jay.

"No," answered Jay curtly. "We just wanted to speak to him."

"He was pushing us around," said Vince, glaring at Stan.

"This sort of thing's no good. What's it all about?"

"Nothing." Jay set his mouth obstinately.

"Nothing?"

"It's private. It's nothing to do with school."

"I see. You two can come and see me in the morning and——"

"It's Saturday," Vince piped up.

"Then that will give you two more days to cool down, won't it?"

"Yes, sir. Good-night, sir." Vince screwed up his face as the master retreated.

Without another word Stan was wheeling out his bike.

"That's done it," said Vince.

"He's not going to get away with it," muttered Jay.

CHAPTER TWENTY-FIVE

MR HENTY GIVES A HAND

"Come on, you two." Mr Lewis stood at the stile by the footpath that led over the last field to Mr Henty's bungalow. The stubble was pale in the wide stretch of land, the surrounding hedge was dark.

Vince was over the hedge first. "D'you reckon he will, Mr Lewis?"

"Who will what?"

Vince laughed. "I reckon he will."

"I reckon we're sunk if he doesn't. Oars cost a tidy bit."

"Couldn't you make them, Dad?"

Mr Lewis shook his head slowly. "Let's say I've never had occasion to try my hand at it."

Mr Henty was seated by the open french window, smoking his pipe. "Well now, what brings you here again?"

"A bit of news—and a bit of a proposition. The last was mine, so don't blame the boys for it."

"Then we'll have the news first."

"It's about *The Henty*," began Jay.

"I've been thinking about *The Henty*. See over there." Mr Henty pointed with the stem of his pipe to the distant scene. "That's the Ander. I can see it on a good day from here. So I think to myself—she's out there—*The Henty*'s afloat, nice little name-board on her for everyone to see."

"Truth is she's had a stormy passage since last we met." Mr Lewis took the chair alongside Mr Henty.

"Oh dear. That's a bad show. But a good boat weathers most things. How did it happen?"

Between them Jay and Vince recounted the story of the loss and the salvage of *The Henty*. Then they related how they had presented her to the club, and there was no doubt that it was this final episode that delighted Mr Henty the most.

"Now I call that a really fine idea," he declared.

"Trouble is, Mr Henty, the boys never found the oars." Mr Lewis looked across at Jay and Vince.

"Now thereby hangs a tale." Mr Henty puffed at his pipe, gazing at the distant scene. "Last summer there were two, sometimes three young fellows, used to come for a bit of fishing. Several times I saw them. They weren't on my land, so nothing wrong in their fishing. Mind you, I'd a good notion they came over the bridge and borrowed my boat, but I never caught them at it." He looked at Jay and Vince.

Jay grinned sheepishly. They had done the same, borrowed *The Henty*.

"One of them had a motor-bike, and they'd ride up and down the path your side of the Ander, but a bit out of your sight. After the holidays I didn't see any more of them. One had a uniform, so I concluded he was either a messenger boy or a tele-graph boy."

Jay looked at Vince.

"Something happened one day; the boat was left downstream, and the oars were missing. I can't prove it was those lads; they didn't show up after that. But there was some sort of trouble among themselves."

"A telegraph boy?" asked Mr Lewis.

"Something like that."

Jay felt himself reddening. There were questions he wanted to ask, but not in front of his father. But were they on to something? Was God answering his prayers?

"So that's how the oars went," continued Mr Henty. "Not being able to get about in her any more, I didn't do anything about it. But Mr Barnard's boys, that's different. And seeing it's *The Henty*, I couldn't allow her to be without oars."

"No," responded Jay. Mr Henty was a sport.

"Mr Barnard's a sensible sort of chap. Suppose I commission him to make the purchase?"

"Yeh." Vince was almost dancing with delight.

"Mind you," Mr Henty looked at them in mock severity, "I want the name on first: *The Henty*— don't forget that."

"We won't forget; it was us named her," said Vince.

CHAPTER TWENTY-SIX

MRS LEWIS ON THE TRAIL

Warm and tired after their walk, they entered the kitchen where Mrs Lewis was preparing tea—a plate of sandwiches, cool cucumber and tomatoes, a dish of plums. It was everything they needed.

"Can Vince stay, Gran?"

"If you'd taken the trouble to look, you'd have seen there's four places set."

Jay made a face. "Might've been for someone else."

"Nonsense."

They sat round the table.

"We're going to have the oars, Gran," said Jay. "Mr Henty thought it was a super idea of ours—you know, giving the boat to the club."

"You mean it was a good idea of your father's." Jay laughed at her, she always had to be so precise. "Oh you can laugh, but it saves a mint of trouble if you always tell the truth, the whole truth."

Jay offered Vince another sandwich, avoiding his grandmother's eyes. The trouble with her was that she had a knack of detecting the truth, even when you devised the cleverest scheme for side-tracking her.

"Yes, he's as pleased as punch to have the boat named *The Henty*." Mr Lewis began slicing the cucumber. "Something very interesting he told us." Jay knew what was coming.

"Wonder he got a chance to say anything with you three there. Now Vince, you help yourself."

Jay listened to his father retailing Mr Henty's story. And he knew his grandmother would make a mental note of the fact that neither he nor Vince made any attempt to tell the incident. It was true she always seemed to spot the truth, and to spot when you weren't telling the truth, but there was one thing he could do of which she was unaware. He could tell when she was working something out, because she continued whatever she happened to be doing only in a more intense manner. Now she was cutting the cake, carefully and exactly slicing each piece as though it helped her to some conclusion.

"Mm." And that was the only comment she made, but it meant she was thinking a great deal more.

Then the subject switched back to the future plans for *The Henty* and Jay began to talk again. Mrs Lewis rose from the table, untied her apron, and, after folding it, laid it neatly over the back of her chair. She didn't so much as glance at Jay or Vince, but spoke to Mr Lewis.

"If you'll get the boys to help you wash up, I think I'll pop along to Mrs Richards for a bit." She closed the kitchen door behind her and the next moment they could hear her steps going down the side passage.

"She's on the warpath." Mr Lewis looked amused, but Jay was too worried to laugh. "And I'll tell you two one thing. If there's anything to be found out from the Richards, Gran will certainly find it."

Vince was a little distrustful of her abilities.

"Now, we'd better start on the table, or we'll be in for a drumming." Mr Lewis pushed back his chair.

Jay disliked washing up intensely. "D'you think she'll be long?"

"No. Once she's got what she went for, she'll be back."

Jay began to stack the plates. Neither Jay nor Vince enquired what it was Mrs Lewis had suddenly found it necessary to see Mrs Richards about. Something in his grandmother's determined air made Jay think that this visit was no ordinary visit. They had barely finished clearing up when she reappeared.

"Well it didn't take long to find that out." She went across to the dresser and wrote on a scrap of paper. Handing it to Jay, she proceeded to make sure that the washing-up had been done to her satisfaction.

Jay read the words slowly: 'Paul Draycott, 2 Bishops Way, Lisham.' Vince hovered nearby.

"Mm. That's your telegraph boy. Lived next door to the Richards when they were in Lisham. Not that he's still a telegraph boy. He's gone up the grade since then."

Then no-one spoke and Jay clutched the paper, half afraid to look at his father. Mrs Lewis shifted china, Vince kept close to Jay, and Mr Lewis watched the two boys.

"Gran," said Jay at last, "how did you find out?" He detected a gleam of pride in her eyes.

"I didn't have to."

"But—you didn't know before."

"No. I didn't know before. There happened to be something she'd been waiting to tell me, something she overheard the other evening."

"Oh." Jay remembered the blue-squared cloth, and Mrs Richards standing by the door.

"Mm. So once we were on the subject of telegrams the rest followed—well, with a bit of encouragement."

"May I have a look, Jay?" Mr Lewis held out his hand for the paper.

"Now listen to me, you two lads." Mrs Lewis rounded on Jay and Vince. "Twenty-four hours I give you; no more. Then I start on this Paul Draycott."

"Gran, you couldn't," objected Jay.

"Couldn't!" Her voice was raised. "That I could. And I'd make sure no-one was eavesdropping. You'll not stop me finding out. So you'd better be quick and do the job yourselves."

"Well, it's up to you." Mr Lewis returned the paper to Jay.

"Come on." Jay nudged Vince. "Thanks, Gran. Oh, was Stan in?"

"No. He was due in for a bit of tea, and then he was off into Lisham with his pals."

"O.K. Thanks."

They chased upstairs and closed the bedroom door.

"What we going to do?" asked Vince.

Jay sat on the edge of the bed. "Dunno. Stan's a rotter. He never answers anything. S'pose we'll have to try the other one."

"No fear!"

"Why not?"

"It wasn't you had him twisting your arm."

"There'd be two of us." Jay eyed Vince. "O.K., we have another go at Stan. We'll catch him as he comes back."

CHAPTER TWENTY-SEVEN

PILLION PASSENGER

Out in Fortune Row, the air was warm with the gentle warmth of September. The windows of the little houses were open, so that Jay and Vince could hear the television news coming from more than one home.

"We'll go down the side," suggested Vince. "Bet he's on his bike, so we'll hear him coming."

Jay agreed.

"Then we'll get him before he knows." Vince scowled. "Serve him right."

That reminded them of Monday, when they were supposed to give an explanation of their attack on Stan.

They passed Stan's house, eyeing the bright red door, the well-ordered front garden, the newly built garage alongside the house. They went a little way down the grassy passage that led to the river, then leant against the garden fence and listened for the approach of the motor-bike. Between the palings of the fence they caught glimpses of the lawn, the new shed, the brilliant dahlias.

Jay wondered how they could force Stan to give in; so far he had resisted everything—the clue of the ring, the threat of delivering other copies, the threat of the post office. Then it came to him in a flash what had put Stan on their trail. It was that Saturday

morning when the photographer was by the tree.
Stan had been hanging around, which was a bit odd.
He must have come for something, and, like them,
found he wasn't alone. And then Vince had shouted,
'He found it first, mister.' Stan had seen him pointing
at Jay. So that was how Stan knew who was first at
the tree, who was most likely to have discovered any
envelopes. And Stan had been watching him ever
since. It all fitted in, even if it didn't explain why the
telegrams were so important to Stan.

His thoughts were interrupted by the sound of the
motor-bike. They chased to the corner and turned
into Fortune Row as the engine ceased its vibration,
ready to challenge their victim. They stopped dead;
once again they were foiled. Stan was not alone; he
had a pillion passenger.

Then Jay had a feeling, a sudden inspiration who
the passenger was. Paul Draycott. Only it didn't
look like Paul Draycott, not how he had pictured him
anyway. Now that he had dismounted you could see
he was shorter than Stan, and he didn't look like the
leader as they had imagined he was.

"Please God," prayed Jay, "help us know what
to do." The words of the psalm, Robinson Crusoe's
psalm, came to him: 'Call upon me in the day of
trouble: I will deliver thee, and thou shalt glorify
me.' It was odd, that last bit; it didn't seem to belong.
Perhaps it was because you liked to think it was you
managed to get out of a fix, even when you asked
God. Was he asking God to help just so that he could
brag afterwards that he'd cornered Stan and Paul?
He knew that was what he wanted to do. Was it
two-parts God helping you, and you saying thank
you? Then that's what he'd do.

"Hallo," he blurted out, facing the two riders. Stan was furious, even more riled than yesterday.

"You lied about us yesterday."

"Get out." Stan looked anxiously at the house.

"We're not going."

"Don't try it on again," threatened Stan.

"We've been to see Mr Henty this afternoon."

"Didn't you hear me tell you to get out?"

"And he told us about last summer. He knows things." Jay looked at Paul; he was sure now that it was Paul, for he looked more alarmed than Stan.

"He knows nothing."

Paul turned to Stan.

"He does." Now Jay assumed a more assured manner and Vince became more bold.

"His dad and his gran know about Paul Draycott." Vince too had jumped to the idea that this was Paul.

"They never saw me," gasped Paul. He was really alarmed.

"Shut up," Stan turned on him.

"And Mr Henty knows about the boat you borrowed and the oars you lost."

Then Paul seemed to recover from his first cringing fear and he turned on Stan. "Look, you carry the can for once. It was you crashed the bike."

"Keep your head, you idiot," retorted Stan; "you don't want to take any notice of kids. What's it to do with me anyway? Who mentioned a crash? Who's asking about a motor-bike?"

"We are," said Jay; "it was the post office bike."

"And I suppose you'd go crawling round with some yarn like the rotten little sneaks you are." Stan was livid.

"It was you borrowed the bike," Paul flared at Stan, "and made me say it was my accident."

"And who delivered telegrams in a tree, just so he could come fishing?" They were at each other's throats, each trying to shift the blame onto the other. "And it's got nothing to do with you infants." Stan was irritated by their presence.

"Oh yes it has," declared Jay. "It has to do with my father. His telegram happened to be very important. He lost a—a business deal."

"Some business deal," scoffed Stan.

Jay's temper was roused. Who did Stan think he was! "He's got things a lot more valuable than your bike." He kicked some pebbles at the offending machine. "There's plenty of others got bikes like yours, but there's not many got what my dad's got. Suppose he had Paul up for not delivering that telegram, than Paul'ud have to go to court——"

"Yeh," Vince butted in; "he'd be in the witness box. I swear to tell the truth, the whole truth——" Vince rolled his eyes upwards in mock solemnity, then he thrust his face forward at Stan, "and he'd have to say about you."

"As it happens I don't intend to prosecute." So engrossed had they been with their own problem, none of them had noticed Mr Lewis approaching. They all turned towards him. "Good evening, Stanley and Paul. I believe God has something to say to us all; more than the few words in the telegram. I'd like to feel you have heard what He has to say."

Paul looked down at the ground. "Thanks," he muttered.

"You're in a bit of trouble, I gather, though I don't know all the ins and outs of it," said Mr Lewis.

"I don't know what'll happen." Paul still didn't look up.

Jay was angry that Stan didn't support his friend; Paul was on his own. He thought of Robinson Crusoe's verse again, but how could he tell someone like Paul about it? If only his father would do it! He was good at that sort of thing; he could explain. But it was his message, and maybe his father didn't even know about it, so he must say it somehow to help Paul.

"I got in a mess about the telegrams too," he admitted, "and Vince, he got like that about the fishing rod."

Vince looked embarrassed.

"Well," Jay fidgeted, "there's this bit in *Robinson Crusoe* Mr Barnard told us about."

"Ah, where Robinson Crusoe finds his Bible; 'Call upon me in the day of trouble: I will deliver thee.' "

"Yeh, that's the bit." Jay was glad of his father's help.

Paul was desperate, no smile on his face. "I could lose my job, and I wouldn't get a reference."

"How did it all happen?" asked Mr Lewis.

Paul glanced at Stan, but got no help. "I used to let them have a go on the bike. Last summer it was. And I went fishing with them. It was seeing them free and me having to work made me do it. Then Stan crashed it on the bridge and that did it. I told them I skidded; it wasn't much damaged, but I had to say it was me or I would have got into worse trouble."

"And what did you say about the telegrams?"

"I said I'd delivered them, and there was no answer. It wasn't very many. I——"

"You delivered them, you say?"

Paul looked up and as soon looked away. "In the tree, the one by the river. It was a bit of fun."

"Which explains a lot. God has strange ways of revealing secrets and delivering messages. I'll tell you what we can do. Suppose you come along with me to see Mr Barnard—we'll talk things over."

"There's the others," interrupted Jay.

"We got them." Vince was cocky.

"That's not what you told me, Jay."

"We opened them all, and copied them," admitted Jay. "Not yours, Dad. I never opened that."

"So Paul and Stanley aren't the only guilty ones."

"My dad won't listen," said Paul hopelessly.

"I can come with you," offered Mr Lewis.

Mrs Richards opened the front door. "Stanley," she called in her sing-song voice. "Oh, it's you, Mr Lewis." She stared at the group.

"That's all right, Mrs Richards. We're just going," said Mr Lewis, and she withdrew. "What about it, Paul? D'you want any help?"

"Guess so. I couldn't tell him on my own."

Stan turned and pushed the bike towards the garage. They watched him disappear out of sight, knowing he was ashamed, the whole incident had shown him up. He wasn't going to stand by Paul. When it meant safeguarding himself he had held to Paul; now he thought it safer to be out of things.

Jay sympathised with Paul. Funny, he wasn't angry with him any more. He thought of the other bit where Robinson Crusoe found there was a worse trouble from which he needed to be rescued. That was how Paul was.

"It was me and Stan sunk the boat," admitted Paul.

"Well, there's quite a story to that. Come on, Paul; we'll go and see Mr Barnard."

Jay and Vince watched them go.

"Wonder what old Barney'll say?" Vince said.

"He'll say it was all *The Henty*. I mean, well it was to be God's boat, so that was why it discovered things. If it hadn't been for *The Henty*, we'd never have gone to see Mr Henty; and if we hadn't given her to the club, we wouldn't have gone to see him again and heard about the telegraph boy. So——"

"Yeh, I reckon it's all up to *The Henty*."

"Hey, Vince, let's go and have a look at *The Henty*."

"Yeh, lets."

AUTHOR'S NOTE

A hollow tree which crashed one August in a North-west London suburb was found to contain a number of undelivered telegrams. It transpired that over a period of months the telegraph boy had used the tree to deposit the telegrams instead of delivering them.

The author never learned how the young man explained his action, nor how he occupied himself when he should have been delivering the telegrams.